SAT
作文滿分攻略
Composition Strategy

鐘莉 ◎編著

仔細閱讀本書，領會SAT作文技巧，
掌握高分祕訣。你也可以拿六分

菘燁文化

SAT 作文滿分攻略

目錄

Chapter III
8 Steps for Writing a Good Essay

Chapter IV
Writing Essays Practice

Chapter V
9 SAT essay Topics and Essay Sample Explanation

Chapter VI
Example sources for SAT

Chapter VII
Quotes and Proverbs

前 言

　　對於很多 SAT 考生來說，作文部分是他們心中的一個「痛」。如何在二十五分鐘時間裡，有效地組織一篇觀點明確、邏輯清晰、論據有說服力的文章是一次挑戰。當然，與此同時，文法要過關，語言的駕馭能力要盡可能充分體現，更重要的是，不能離題。面對這個看似不可完成的任務，多少考生在困惑，在迷茫。滿分六分，或許是個遙不可及的夢。

　　然而，告訴大家一個秘密：寫好作文是有章可循的。你不能預知考題題目，但是你可以獲知的是：如何為寫作文打基礎，做準備；如何搜集素材，建立自己的「論據庫」；如何選擇自己的立場並使論據與此緊密相連；如何支配時間；如何使文章出彩。總而言之，如果你為六分做好了準備，六分就會在不遠處等著你。所以，不要在心裡與它說再見，告訴自己：你可以。畢竟，作文占據寫作部分三分之一的成績，你的付出是值得的。同時你該知道，為作文做準備，目的不僅僅是作文成績本身，準備與練習作文的過程更是一個磨練自己邏輯思維能力與辯理能力的過程，它使人終生受益，這也是 SAT 美國大學考試委員會添加作文的原因之一。

　　為此，仔細閱讀本書，領會 SAT 作文技巧，掌握高分秘訣。你也可以拿六分。

One of the most frequently asked SAT essay questions from my students is that "How can I improve my essay writing?" or in other words, "I know it's hard, but how can I get full score or at least five?" To many students, writing an essay is a frustrating and even exasperating process. They feel baffled by the task and consider what they would have to do is to swallow the animosity towards writing. The reason the students have such doubts about writing or they are reluctant to write is that they are not ready and they don't know HOW to get ready.

If you understand how to prepare for an SAT essay, writing can be easy and getting a perfect score is a "mission possible".

In this book you will learn how to prepare for an SAT essay and how to improve your writing skills through the following techniques:

- 7 Tips for maximizing your score
- 8 Steps for completing your essay
- 9 Essay topics with sample essay explanations
- Essay example sources and aphorisms you need to know

Chapter I

SAT essay Overview

　　所謂「知己知彼，百戰百勝」，SAT 作文亦是如此。考作文前你需要做何準備？是誰為你的作文評分？四分與五分的差別在哪裡，五分與六分的評分標準區別在何處？是否一定要使用印刷體寫作文？透徹理解 SAT 作文要求，是你邁向成功的第一步。

　　The SAT Reasoning Test is a standardized test, which is required for college admissionby many colleges and universities in the United States. Since it was first introduced in 1901, its name and scoring have changed several times. The current SAT, administeredin March of 2005, includes three major sections: writing, mathematics and criticalreading. And each major section consists of three sub-sections. Together with an additional experimental section, which may be in any of the three question types and will not count toward your final score, there are 10 sections. Essay topic, as one of the three writing sections, will be the first part you face when you sit down to take the SAT.

What you need to know before you write

SAT essay is 25 minutes in length

　　A student is given 25 minutes to complete an essay, which seems to be a maddening task to many. When essay part was first added to writing section as one of the big changes to the new version of SAT in 2005, most students claimed that they did not think an essay set in 25 minutes on a topic which they could not prepare for collecting materials would be commensurate with their skills.

Ed Hardin, a College Board test specialist responded, "We know students don't write well when they're anxious. We don't want them not to go forward with that little detail. Our attitude is to go right ahead with the missing date and readers should be instructed not to count off for that."

"Writing is a requirement for doing well in college and doing well in life," Gaston Caperton, the eighth president of the College Board said, "And we are proud that we put writing on this."

In fact, the SAT essay is not designed to test "how well you write" . It is designed to test how well-and rapidly-you orient yourself to a new topic, organize your thoughts, develop your ideas, think logically and write the first draft of a persuasive essay.

Right, it's still difficult with only 25 minutes to construct a piece of article in rush and it has to be well organized, creatively written with good command of language skills. But don't worry; fortunately, there are ways to make it easier. As long as you read the book and follow the instructions, you should be well on your way in acing your SAT essay in 25 minutes.

Use pencil

Do not use a pen. An essay written in pen will be marked zero.

College Board has made it very clear that test takers must use a No. 2 pencil only and they may not use a pen or mechanical pencil.

There are some students in my class who used to write essays in mechanical pencils. They complained that they use mechanical pencils almost every day and mechanical pencil makes the writing a lot clearer for precision and why it would matter much to write in mechanical pencil.

In fact, No. 2 pencil is also called HB ("H" stands for hardness of the lead, and

"B" for blackness of the pencil's mark). Since the essay will be scanned and No. 2 lead, which is hard and black enough, is what the scantron best detects, there is no need to make a risk. So don't score a zero for failing to follow guidelines.

Write legibly

Handwriting seems to become a lost art in the age of computer. However, having good handwriting can help you in school and beyond.

If you don't think you can turn to be the one who has good handwriting in a short period of time, at least write legibly.

Legible writing is a valuable thing, which involves the readability of letters, as well as spacing within and between words.

When given 25 minutes for an essay, it is easy to let your handwriting look sloppy and messy. But keep in mind that essay graders read hundreds of essays each day. If you don't write legibly, they will not bother to spend more time than required to think of deciphering what you write. The truth is if your script is hard to decipher, your score would probably be lowered. Do yourself a favor and write legibly.

No "right" or "wrong" answer to topic assignment

In the SAT essay portion, the test taker is presented with a prompt in the form of a question or statement, and asked to write an essay about it.

There is no right or wrong answer to the question; the test taker is expected to analyze the issue, address the important sides of the issue and offer examples to support his or her position. Because there is no one "correct" answer, the individual will be scored onhis or her ability to organize the arguments and defend the position he or she stands for.

Scores will increase for those who demonstrate complex arguments with logic and clarity and those who exhibit skillful use of language.

Who are the readers?

Each essay will be scored independently by two readers from the College Board. The readers, or graders, are usually college or high school teachers who have been teaching writing or English for a minimum of three years. Before they are given the essays, they would have extensive training provided by the College Board.

Meanwhile, the College Board has collaborated with Pearson Educational Measurementto recruit experienced teachers or people who meet their qualifications to read and score the essay almost every year. Readers will work from their homes or offices with online scoring system.

How are the essays graded?

Each reader will assign the essay a score ranging from 1 to 6. Their scores are added together to give a final score of up to 12 points. Essays not written will receive a score of zero. If the two readers' scores differ by more than one point, a third reader will score the essay.

The essay score counts for 1/3 of your score on the Writing section and 1/9 of your total SAT score.

What are the scoring criteria?

According to College Board, your essay will be graded "holistically" , which means thegraders would take everything in the paper into account:

They will rate your ability to develop and express a point of view in response to the topic, your ability to use examples, logic, critical thinking and reasoning to support your position, and your skill in language competency.

Graders read quickly. A grader may be asked to grade more than 250 essays every day in an eight hour shift. This means a grader spends only two or two and a half minutes on each essay on average.

So holistically, in other words, also means that graders read very quickly for an impression of the whole paper and then score immediately. As a result, your essay's score will be based in some way on the first impressions formed by two graders.

Following is the scoring criteria (source: www.collegeboard.com). Use the criteria to analyze the sample essays and analyze why some deserve a high score while others not. This also helps you to judge what is missing in your essay so that you can improve your essay writing.

An essay in this category demonstrates clear and consistent mastery, although it may have a few minor errors. A typical essay:

► Effectively and insightfully develops a point of view on the issue anddemonstrates outstanding critical thinking, using clearly appropriate examples, reasons and other evidence to support its position

► Is well organized and clearly focused, demonstrating clear coherence and smooth progression of ideas

► Exhibits skillful use of language, using a varied, accurate and apt vocabulary

► Demonstrates meaningful variety in sentence structure

► Is free of most errors in grammar, usage and mechanics

An essay in this category demonstrates reasonably consistent mastery, although it has occasional errors or lapses in quality. A typical essay:

► Effectively develops a point of view on the issue and demonstrates strong critical thinking, generally using appropriate examples, reasons and othe revidence to support its position

► Is well organized and focused, demonstrating coherence and progression of ideas

► Exhibits facility in the use of language, using appropriate vocabulary

► Demonstrates variety in sentence structure

▶ Is generally free of most errors in grammar, usage and mechanics

An essay in this category demonstrates adequate mastery, although it has lapses in quality. A typical essay:

▶ Develops a point of view on the issue and demonstrates competent critical thinking, using adequate examples, reasons and other evidence to support its position

▶ Is generally organized and focused, demonstrating some coherence and progression of ideas

▶ Exhibits adequate but inconsistent facility in the use of language, using generally appropriate vocabulary

▶ Demonstrates some variety in sentence structure

▶ Has some errors in grammar, usage and mechanics

An essay in this category demonstrates developing mastery, and is marked by ONE OR MORE of the following weaknesses:

▶ Develops a point of view on the issue, demonstrating some critical thinking, but may do so inconsistently or use inadequate examples, reasons or other evidence to support its position

▶ Is limited in its organization or focus, or may demonstrate some lapses in coherence or progression of ideas

▶ Displays developing facility in the use of language, but sometimes uses weak vocabulary or inappropriate word choice

▶ Lacks variety or demonstrates problems in sentence structure

▶ Contains an accumulation of errors in grammar, usage and mechanics

An essay in this category demonstrates little mastery, and is flawed by ONE OR MORE of the following weaknesses:

▶ Develops a point of view on the issue that is vague or seriously limited, and demonstrates weak critical thinking, providing inappropriate or insufficient examples, reasons or other evidence to support its position

▶ Is poorly organized and/or focused, or demonstrates serious problems with coherence or progression of ideas

▶ Displays very little facility in the use of language, using very limited vocabulary or incorrect word choice

▶ Demonstrates frequent problems in sentence structure

▶ Contains errors in grammar, usage and mechanics so serious that meaning is somewhat obscured

An essay in this category demonstrates very little or no mastery, andis severely flawed by ONE OR MORE of the following weaknesses:

▶ Develops no viable point of view on the issue, or provides little or no evidence to support its position

▶ Is disorganized or unfocused, resulting in a disjointed or incoherent essay Displays fundamental errors in vocabulary

▶ Demonstrates severe flaws in sentence structure

▶ Contains pervasive errors in grammar, usage or mechanics that persistently interfere with meaning

Essays not written on the essay assignment will receive a score of zero.

Chapter II

7 Tips to Know for Maximizing Your Score

「愛心得匠意，則傑作在望。」如何做好 SAT 作文的準備工作呢？態度首先決定一切。對於 SAT 作文來說，積極樂觀充滿「愛」的態度好比天使的翅膀，為你的寫作推波助瀾。此外，你需要培養良好的閱讀習慣，建立並充實你的例證「素材庫」，隨時為各種題目做好「戰前」準備，當然，你還需要知道怎樣才可以「打動」讀者——你的評分人。紀伯倫說過：「如果你要寫作，必須要有知識、藝術和魔術。」具體到 SAT，知識便指你的例證素材（或言，你平時對閱讀知識的積累）；藝術指你的語言魅力；魔術，則是熱愛你的讀者和如何打動你的讀者的技巧和力量。閱讀本章闡述的七個高分作文技巧，為成功做好準備。

As a SAT test taker, you hope your essay would demonstrate your ability in organization, argument, critical thinking and language competency. You only have 25 minutes, and you only have probably no more than 400 words to show what you are capable of in writing. How to use the best of the limit time to show to your readers and convince them that you deserve the best score of writing seems to be a difficult task. However, nothing in the world is impossible if you set your mind on it. If you learn how to prepare for your essay, you will be only a step away from success.

Tip one: Attitude decides everything
-be positive over negative

"Writing SAT essay is so frustrating a job to do." If this is what you think every time before you sit down and write the essay, you are minimizing your score rather than maximizing it.

Writing can be fun and it is a skill not only for SAT, but also for your daily life in the future. This is also why College Board added essay to writing section in 2005. They know writing is a good way to stimulate learning and critical thinking and writing skills are essential for succeeding in high school, college, and on the job.

Officials from the College Board also described essay writing as a tool that could transform American education, forcing schools to better teach writing in 2005. Time magazine even said, it "is a great social experiment".

Now read the following quotes and try to understand the attitude writers have about writing.

"It is necessary to write, if the days are not to slip emptily by. How else, indeed, to clap the netover the butterfly of the moment? For the moment passes, it is forgotten; the mood is gone; lifeitself is gone. That is where the writer scores over his fellows: he catches the changes of his mind on the hop."

-- *Vita Sackville-West, English writer and poet*

"Writing became such a process of discovery that I couldn't wait to get to work in the morning: I wanted to know what I was going to say. "

-- *Sharon O'Brien, freelance writer*

"The act of putting pen to paper encourages pause for thought, this in turn makes us think more deeply about life, which helps us regain our equilibrium."

-- *Norbet Platt, CEO from a German company.*

Feeling inspired? Attitude isn't everything when it comes to being successful, but attitude plays a part in every phase of your life. Your attitude towards SAT essay would decide what and how much you prepare for the writing.

In life, there are at least two ways to look at virtually everything. A pessimist looks for difficulty in the opportunity, whereas an optimist looks for opportunity in the difficulty. William Black, a novelist from Scotland said, "Two men looked out from prison bars. One saw mud, the other saw stars."

Unfortunately, some people look only at the difficulty, not realizing that if you think positively about the essay writing, look at the situation from a new angle, you could put your heart to get more prepared for the essay, and you would be likely to be more close to a high score.

Or, you can tell yourself; it is better to change one's attitude than to change one circumstance. You can't do anything to change the fact that the SAT essay requires you to complete an essay in a 25-minute time limit, but you can do a great deal to learn to practice and prepare for the essay. You're guaranteed a better score tomorrow by doing your best today and develop a plan of preparation for tomorrows that lie ahead. Just to maintain a positive mental attitude so that, as you prepare for essay, you're doing sowith sense of expectancy that produces substantially better results.

Tip two: Cultivate good reading habits
-take notes while reading

In China there is a common saying that if you can recite 300 poems of Tang Dynasty, you can compose poems, too. It tells us the important relationship between reading and writing: reading is good for writing.

We do not learn how to speak by speaking alone, but by listening to the people around us use language every day and gradually picking up the rules. Similarly, we do not learn to be good writers just by writing, but by studying the writings of greater and more experienced writers than ourselves. The more great writing you read and the more intensely you interact with it, the more your own writing will improve.

Reading will help you internalize the structure, strengthen your grammar, and through reading, one can get exposure of various styles of writing and from that you can create your own unique style of writing.

Here are five steps for improving your writing skills while reading.

1. Create a reading list

Create a reading list. Make sure you can see the list no matter where you are. The list includes every book you want to read. If you don't know where to begin, you can read the bestseller lists to gain some suggestions, or investigate award-winning authors and books. Awards such as the Nobel Prize in Literature, the Pulitzer Prize, the National Book Award signify worthy literary accomplishments. Classic books, which have excellent language usage and deep messages, would also help you improve writing skills while reading.

Of course you can read books that you enjoy. Don't ignore a book just because it hasn't made it into the list of classics. You can learn a lot from nearly any type of writing that appeals to you.

What's more, the reading list can be updated: when you find a good book online or from others, add it; if you finish reading a book, delete it from your reading list.

2. Think while reading

Good reading habits require clear thinking. Clear thinking helps improve writing.

Clear thinking is the process of digesting contents. It is a way of learning what you read. While reading, you should think logically, analyze and compare, question and evaluate, draw inferences and arrive at conclusions based on the content you read. Without thinking, reading is no difference of gadgets or on-line games exposed to the students.

In fact, this is the aim of SAT as well. They want students to be taught to be critical thinkers, critical readers and creative writers. To think clearly and effectively, students must read analytically and accurately. They must write their thoughts with a solid command of vocabulary, sentencing, and organizing content. Vice versa, the more clearly and logically they think when they read, the better they will perform while writing.

Elbow, P. (1983) has presented a two-step writing process called first-order and second-order thinking. For first-order thinking, he recommends free writing an unplanned, free-association type of heuristic writing designed to help students discover what they think about a topic. The free writing technique produces conceptual insights. Elbow asked students to write a few incidents that came to mind without careful thinking. This resulted in more intuitive, creative thinking. Elbow cautions that the reflective scrutiny of second-order thinking is a necessary follow-up of free writing. In this stage, the writer examines inferences and prejudices and strives for logic andcontrol.

(For more information: Elbow, P. "Teaching Thinking by Teaching Writing" .)

3. Take notes while reading

Taking note is an important tool that reinforces the book your read. It is also a processof critical thinking. Stop at every chapter or even a couple of times every chapter totake down some notes. Write what happens in the book, what you like and what you don't like, how the writer made his point and what you think inspires you.

You would probably disagree with the writer's opinion; you may think arguments in a book may be based on inaccurate, unreliable or obsolete evidence, and may ignore any evidence against those arguments; you have maybe read newspaper reports that seem biased or lack supporting evidence. In this case, you can write down your opinions on your notebook. This is a good way to improve your reading skills as well as your writing skills as the SAT essay tasks ask you to take a position and use examples or evidence to support your standing point.

Also, every time you come across a word you like, write down the word, the definition and the sentence it is used in the book. This will help you learn new words for use in your own writing.

So effective note taking can help you keep motivated and concentrated while you study, improve your language skills, better your understanding by making you read actively and critically, internalize difficult ideas by putting them into your own words, and organize your ideas in preparation for writing, leading to fuller, better connected arguments in your essays.

But while taking notes remember not to take notes all the time and don't try to take remember everything you read. Of course don't be concerned about whether anyone else could make sense of your handwriting; you're the only one who needs to readthem. You can try different ways of taking notes. Try lists, colors, bullet points, underlining, highlighting and mind mapping. Experimenting with various methods helps you discover the technique that suits you.

As a result, the more you interact with the book, the more you will learn from it.

4. Reading is pleasure

Reading is pleasure of the mind. But reading can only be fun if you expect it to be. If you tell yourself reading is just for an examination like SAT, or you read because others such as your teachers ask you to do, you probably won't have fun. Instead, if you have positive attitude toward reading: "The more you read, the more things you will know. The more that you learn, the more places you'll go." As Dr. Seuss said in "I can Read With My Eyes Shut!" or "We read to know we are not alone," by C.S. Lewis, you will have a good time, as Anthony Trollope said "The habit of reading is the only enjoyment in which there is no alloy; it lasts when all other pleasures fade."

Also remember, the most unfortunate people in the world are probably those who have never discovered how satisfying it is to read good books.

If this is not enough to show the pleasure of reading, try this: when you are reading,make you a cup of tea, or get you a cup of coffee, sit in a comfortable chair, choose the time you like. You can make reading the best moment of a day.

Tip three: Examples, examples and examples -make a summary of example resource

As we know, essay writing will measure the capacity of the students to compose effective essays that will expose their abilities to deliver ideas, communicate efficiently and build reasoning by citing appropriate examples. And one secret to writing an excellent SAT essay and earning a high score from the SAT graders is to write strong,well-structured, and convincing SAT essay examples. Once you've chosen your position,you need to support your argument with powerful examples.

1. Make a list of examples

Like reading list, you need to make a list of examples. But different from the reading list, you have to make a detailed categorized one. This means that the list would composeat least ten different subjects such as literature, history, politics, geography, military, personal experience, etc. (for more detail, please read Chapter VI). Therefore, before writing your SAT essay, you already come up with at least ten possible examples to support your thesis. Think of as many examples as possible from history and literature, as the graders tend to be more impressed with these kinds of examples than with those that come from personal experience.

Bacon said, "Histories make men wise; poets witty; the mathematics subtle; natural philosophy deep; moral grave; logic and rhetoric able to contend." So don't take the task intimidating, making a list of examples not only helps you prepare for SAT, but also helps you become a learned person during the journey of preparation. It would have a lifetime beneficial effect and value to you.

2. Read the news

Besides reading books, you can also choose some newspapers or magazines as examples sources. Read articles from sources like The Wall Street Journal or the NewYork Times to catch up on current events. If you read regularly, current events are an excellent source for essay examples.

Newspaper editorials are also good choices because they usually state a problem and take a position on it, in the space of about 400 to 500 words.

3. Practice arguing by using examples

There are many SAT essay prompts online. Choose three prompts and run a conversation through your head and pretend you're trying to prove a point to someone by using the examples you collected. Your goal on the SAT essay should be to convince the reader that you are right. If you were arguing with someone, what would he say?What would you tell him to disprove his statements?

4. Vary the sources of examples

Try to vary the sources of your SAT essay examples by picking examples from different category. Perhaps pick one from history, one from politics, and one from literature.

5. Can I use song or Harry Potter examples?

In my SATclass, students once ask if they could use song lyrics or Harry Potter or movies like Spiderman, Lord of the Rings as examples. The answer is you can give any examples as long as they are strong examples and strengthen your argument.

But there is something else you should know: when you give political and historical examples, which do not relate to America and not well-known outside your country, give some background information so that the grader is not in the dark. A student in my class once gave an example of Lei Feng, who is a well-known national hero of 1960s in China. His portrait is found on the wall of classroom in the West Point Military Academy and adored by the military people of the United States. However, few other people knew his name in America. The student didn't give enough background about the figure, making her argument less persuasive.

Tip four: Write long
-one and a half pages at least

"Write long" is the most frequently cited advice seen about the SAT essay.

Dr. Les Perelman, one of the directors of undergraduate writing at Massachusetts Institute of Technology, said to New York Times in 2005, "It appeared to me that regardless of what a student wrote, the longer the essay, the higher the score."

Dr. Perelman studied every graded sample SAT essay that the College Board made public. He looked at the 15 samples in the Score Write book that the College Board distributed to high schools nationwide to prepare students for the new writing section. He reviewed the 23 graded essays on the College Board Web site meant as a guide forstudents and the 16 writing "anchor" samples the College Board used to train graders to properly mark essays.

He was stunned by how complete the correlation was between length and score. "I have never found a quantifiable predictor in 25 years of grading that was anywhere near as strong as this one," he said, "If you just graded them based on length without ever reading them, you'd be right over 90 percent of the time." The shortest essays, typically 100 words, got the lowest grade of one. The longest, about 400 words, got the top grade of six. In between, there was virtually a direct match between length and grade.

Early news reports suggested that SAT readers might take less than a minute to judge each essay. Dan Verner, a former English teacher at James W. Robinson Secondary School in Fairfax County, now one of the College Board graders of

SAT, told Washington Post that the actual time per essay is closer to two and a half minutes.

Dr. Perelman is now adept at rapid-fire SAT grading. When reporter of New York Times held up a sample essay far enough away so it could not be read, he was still able to guess the correct grade by its bulk and shape. "That's a 4," he said, "It looks like a 4."

And, although one of the scoring criteria from College Board on SAT essay is: "Do not judge a paper by its length; some short papers are good, and some long papers are poor," a strong correlation between long essays and high scores has been found.

Or, thinking from another angle, since your essay will be graded "holistically" , which is a euphemism for very, very quickly, in all likelihood; each grader will spend at most two and a half minutes on your essay. Unlike your classroom teachers, your two SAT graders don't have the time to appreciate the brilliant nuances of your thinking or to savor your wonderful prose style. Each SAT grader has hundreds of essays to mark aday. As a result, your essay's score will be based entirely on the first impressions, and sometimes, length would be a factor of your score.

For one thing, problems with short essays, defined as little as 100 to 150 words were more likely lack of content or an undeveloped argument.

But remember one thing, longer essays don't guarantee you a high score, but guarantee you free of low score if you are not off the topic. If you can not come up witha coherent response to the prompt, writing long may cut your losses. At least you'll show more of your command of written English. However, a complete, concise essay is always going to score higher than a rambling, long one.

Tip five: Use big words
-don't go overwhelmed

It is true that English teachers often tell students not to use big words as they are goingto be interested in whether or not your ideas support your topic and flow smoothly through the essay. But for SAT essay, graders will also assess your ability of language. A few well-placed big words can have a strong impact on the graders of your SAT essay.

1. Use big words appropriately

But do remember to compose your essay with the goal of showing what you know, not showing off. Trust your vocabulary: don't go overboard, and don't use "big words" if you're unsure of their meanings. In other words, use "big words" appropriately.

2. 66 words that impress SAT graders

The following list emphasizes those SAT words that you may work into just about any assigned essay topic.

The list is compiled from the words professional writers use most often when writing persuasive essays. It isn't intended to be complete. Examine any editorial piece in your local newspaper and you'll find at least one word, or a variation of it, from this list. This list gives special weight to the rhetorical concepts that occur most frequently in SAT essays.

- aberrant
- lethargic
- acute
- momentous
- acrimonious
- notably
- aesthetic

- notion
- altruism
- nuance
- anachronism
- objectivity
- apathy
- orthodox

- aspiration
- omnipotent
- assess
- paradox
- coherent
- perceptive
- contentious
- plausible
- cordial
- plethora
- credulity
- predominant
- depict
- premise
- diabolical
- presumably
- discrepancy
- prodigious
- dogmatic
- proponent
- dubious
- quintessential
- empathy
- realm
- elicit
- relentless

- empirical
- reminiscent
- enduring
- remorse
- epitome
- resolution
- ephemeral
- rhetorical
- exemplify
- scrutiny
- explicit
- secular
- feasible
- skeptic
- ideology
- succinct
- immutable
- transcend
- implication
- ubiquitous
- inherent
- unequivocal
- intrinsic
- utopia
- lament
- vapid

But don't think you have to use every word on this list. Just try to include a few of these words in your essay. These words are especially effective in the first and last paragraphs of SAT essays, which the graders read most carefully.

Tip six: be direct
-avoid wordiness

Brevity is the soul of wit. Come to the point. Don't beat around the bush.

I often read essays, which include vague ideas when making a position. In other words, they don't express themselves in ways that readers understand. Most of the time, it's not because they use too few words to make others understand, but because they use too many.

You should find the right word and use it, and when you make a point, come to it and be direct.

Also, try to keep your writing as simple as possible, avoiding over wordiness.

G. H. Hemingway, son of Ernest Hemingway, showed his novel to his father. Father said it was well written except for one mistake. He pointed to the sentence, "All of a sudden he realized he could fly," and said to his son, "Change 'all of a sudden' into 'suddenly'and never use more words than you have to-it detracts from the flow of actions."

Yes, the general principle is simple: if you've heard a phrase more than a couple of times, and it isn't key wording, essential in carrying meaning, or a definitive phrase, try to get rid of it. While you work on that one, you can dump words like actually, basically, definitely, really, truly, very, always, everything.

a lot of = many, much

absolute unique = unique

all of a sudden = suddenly

all of these = these

almost never = seldom

as a matter of fact = in fact

as a way to = to

at the present time = currently, now

at the same time that = while

based in large part on = based on

because of the fact of = because of

being that = because

both of these/them/the = both

by means of = by

carefully scrutinize = scrutinize

combined together = combined

come to an abrupt end = end abruptly

complete stranger = stranger

completely eliminate = eliminate

deliberately choose = choose

despite the fact that = although

did not succeed = failed

due to the fact that = because

during the course of = during

end result = result

enter into = enter

erode away = erode

few in number = few

first and foremost = first

for the purpose of = to, for

future plans = plans

general public = public

give an indication of = indicate

grouped together = grouped

has the ability to = can

has the opportunity to = can

hear the sound of = hear the

in a situation in which = in

in connection with = about

in spite of the fact that = although

in the final analysis = finally

in the not too distant future = soon

in today's society = today

in view of the fact that = because

large in size = large

mainly focuses on = focuses on

make a decision = decide

make an assumption = assume

mix together = mix

mutual agreement = agreement

natural instinct = instinct

new initiatives = initiatives

on account of the fact that = because

on top of all this = moreover

over and over again = repeatedly

past experience = experience

past history = history

regardless of the fact that = although

refer back = refer

scrutinize carefully = scrutinize

serious crisis = crisis

small-sized = small

shout loudly = shout

the reason why = the reason, why, because

total annihilation = annihilation

totally obvious = obvious

united as one = united

ultimate conclusion = conclusion

what I mean is = I mean

Tip seven: Entertain your reader -add fun to your essay

Humor can be very effective in communicating your ideas in a memorable way. Adding a touch of humor might help impress the reader and would earn you a high score. Incorporating an ounce of sense of humor in your writing will automatically connect you to your readers.

1. Don't be too personal

Of course, humor doesn't necessarily mean throwing a random joke in between paragraphs. You should know when to add humor and when not to. Make sure you do not go over board and become too personal with your readers.

2. Humor impresses readers

Adding humor can be a difficult task for students writing SAT essays in a short time. However, if you want to create an impact on your essay, adding humor could just do the trick. You may add quotes and anecdotes to grab the attention of your readers who will read more than 200 essays and would easily fall into boredom each day.

Also, SAT essay topics are serious and heavy, sometimes. Using humor in this situation, you can make even the headiest materials more palatable, as it provides temporary relief to let them gather their wits.

Chapter III

8 Steps for Writing a Good Essay

　　想拿高分，要先做到一點——不要離題。換言之，一定要準確、清晰地表達自己的立場或者觀點。比如「失敗與成功哪個更有價值？」你的觀點或者是「失敗更有價值」，或者是「成功的價值更高」。但是，如果你只是說「失敗也很重要」，那麼你的角度已經發生了偏差——你根本沒有回答這個問題。如果題目是「失敗也很有價值嗎」，那麼你闡述「失敗也很重要」則是正確的。事實上，很多考生急於下筆寫文，最終因審題失誤而顆粒無收。所以，一定要看清題目，準確、直接地回答問題。此外，想要奪取高分，還需要在邏輯思維與文章架構及語言能力上做出最佳表現。

You want to get a high score of essay. But knowing what exactly the graders are looking for from your essay would help you to achieve the goal. Here is the four perspectives graders base on when judging your essays.

1. Positioning: The strength and clarity of your stance on the given topic.

2. Examples: The relevance and development of the examples you use to support your argument.

3. Organization: The organization of each of your paragraphs and of your essay overall.

4. Language: Sentence construction, grammar, and word choice.

The question is how you can demonstrate your ability of the four perspectives when writing your essay. In what comes, there are eight steps for writing an essay.

Step one: Decide your position
-read the prompt carefully

Time: 3 minutes

First, the assignment should be read in its entirety. Each essay question on the SAT testis accompanied by a paragraph that discusses the issue in question. This paragraph contains important information about the issue, and this information should be taken into account in answering the question.

Here is a sample prompt.

Directions: Consider carefully the following statement and the assignment below it. Then plan and write an essay that explains your ideas as persuasively as possible. Keep in mind that the support you provide-both reasons and examples-will help make your view convincing to the reader.

In his poem, "To a Mouse," the Scottish poet Robert Burns (1759-1796) wrote these immortal lines: "The best laid schemes o' mice an' men / Gang aft a-gley." To paraphrase Burns's archaic dialect in modern English: No matter how carefully weplan our projects, something can still go wrong with them.

Assignment: Are even our best plans always at the mercy of unexpected, chance events? Plan and write an essay in which you develop your point of view on this idea. Support your position with reasoning and examples from your reading, studies, experience, or observations.

Read the prompt several times until you fully comprehend what the topic is about. This may sound like something ridiculously obvious and easy to do, but once you begin answering the question it's surprisingly easy to get off topic.

The second thing you need to do is to decide whether you are pro or con: you must respond to the assigned topic; you must choose YES or NO.

However, one of the biggest problems test takers face is prompts often deal with abstract conflicts that are hard to get worked up about. But keep in mind that you're being graded on your ability to state an argument and to support it. You have to take a stand. Train yourself to do that. An option is to re-state the prompt question in a way that makes it easier to respond to.

Also remember though your instinct might be to support the side that you agree with, this should not be the determining factor. Instead, choose the side that you could more easily support with both argument and examples.

You may think three minutes for reading and deciding your side are too long, but spending some minutes in organizing your thoughts and outlining your answer will allow you to write much faster. Once you get started, you won't have to stop mid-essay to think what to say next because you'll already know. Students who start writing without planning quickly find that their writing has run out of steam. By then it's too late for them to get a fresh start on their essays.

Analyzing prompts practice

Read the writing prompts and answer the following questions.

Directions: Consider carefully the following statement and the assignment below it. Then plan and write an essay that explains your ideas as persuasively as possible. Keep in mind that the support you provide-both reasons and examples-will help make your view convincing to the reader.

Aside from the disastrous effects of emails and chatting on the spelling, grammar and punctuation of the English language, these modern conveniences also considerably affect our personal lives.

Assignment: What is your view of the opinion that the temporary, impersonal nature of modern tools like electronic mail and instant messaging programs are gradually rendering our lives equally temporary and impersonal? Plan and write anessay in which you develop your point of view on this idea. Support your position with reasoning and examples from your reading, studies, experience, or observations.

What is the issue of the excerpt as stated?

What are you supposed to write about the issue?

_____

If you are asked to write an essay to respond to the question, what would your opinion be? Write your position in one sentence.

_____

What examples would you use to support your position? Write down three of them.

Example 1:

_____

Example 2:

_____

Example 3:

_____

Write the source of the idea-for example, a magazine you read or a TV show you watched.

Source of Example 1:

_____

Source of Example 2:

_____

Source of Example 3:

_____

Answers and Explanations

1. The issue is stated in the question: "the temporary, impersonal nature of modern tools like electronic mail and instant messaging programs are gradually rendering ourlives equally temporary and impersonal."

2. What you are supposed to write is stated in the questions also: "your opinion of the idea that the temporary, impersonal nature of modern tools like electronic mail and instant messaging programs are gradually rendering our lives equally

temporary and impersonal."

3. Your sentence should state whether you agree or disagree with the issue as stated in the question. That is: "the temporary, impersonal nature of modern tools like electronic mail and instant messaging programs are gradually rendering our lives equally temporary and impersonal," or "the temporary, impersonal nature of modern tools like electronic mail and instant messaging programs are not gradually rendering our lives equally temporary and impersonal."

4. Analyze the three examples you write to see if they are closely related to the position you pick and if they support your opinion powerfully.

5. Do you have a variety of examples to support your position? Are they all from TV shows or books you read? Remember variety of sources is important. You should try to find different sources: evidence from the same source (for example, your personal experience) may not impress the readers.

More prompts for practice

Read the following prompts and assignment. The directions are not repeated each time. Pick your position and list three examples that are from different source category such as history, literature, current events, TV, magazine or your personal experience. Think of one quote to support your stand also: quotes when used appropriately would impress the graders and make your essay shine.

Directions: Consider carefully the following statement and the assignment below it. Then plan and write an essay that explains your ideas as persuasively as possible. Keep in mind that the support you provide-both reasons and examples-will help make your view convincing to the reader.

1. Forgiveness is the sweetest revenge.

-Isaac Friedmann

Assignment: What is your view of the idea that it is better to forgive than to revenge in one's life? Plan and write an essay in which you develop your point of view on this issue. Support your position with reasoning and examples taken from your reading, studies, experience, or observations.

Issue:

_____

My position:

_____

Example 1:

_____

Source:

_____

Example 2:

_____

Source:

_____

Example 3:

_____

Source:

_____

A quote I may use:

_____

2. The advent of online social networking sites like Myspace and Face-

book is changing the average number of friends people have. Past research by Professor Robin Dunbar at the Evolutionary Psychology and Behavioural Ecology Research Group at Liverpool University has shown that the average person has a social network of around 150 friends, ranging from very close friends to casual acquaintances. Making friends can be costly. While it might not be a very romanticview of friendship, making new friends involves an investment by committing time and energy to another person in the hope that they will provide reciprocal benefits in the future.

Assignment: What is your view of the idea that online social networking is very likely to change the real meaning of friendship? Plan and write an essay in which you develop your point of view on this issue. Support your position with reasoning and examples taken from your reading, studies, experience, or observations.

Issue:

My position:

Example 1:

Source:

Example 2:

Source:

_____

Example 3:

_____

_____

Source:

_____

A quote I may use:

_____

3. The study of ecology has taught us that diversity is important to stability in the natural world. Modern agricultural practices and other human interventions in the environment reduce the number of interacting species making the ecosystem vulnerable and unstable.

Assignment: What is your view of the idea that human society in its progresstoward the clichéd "global village" is liable to make the world less stable not more stable? Plan and write an essay that develops your point of view on the issue.

Support your opinion with reasoning and examples from your reading, your class work, your personal experiences, or your observations.

Issue:

_____

My position:

_____

Example 1:

_____

_____

Source:

_____

Example 2:

_____

_____

Source:

_____

Example 3:

_____

_____

Source:

_____

A quote I may use:

_____

_____

4. Much of what goes by the name of pleasure is simply an effort to destroy consciousness. If one started by asking, what is man? What are his needs? How can he best express himself? One would discover that merely having the power to avoid work and live one's life from birth to death in electric light and to the tune oftinned music is not a reason for doing so.

Assignment: Does human being's highest happiness lie in seeking pleasure or in hard work? Plan and write an essay in which you develop your point of view on this issue. Support your position with reasoning and examples taken from your reading, studies, experience, or observations.

Issue:

_____

My position:

Example 1:

Source:

Example 2:

Source:

Example 3:

Source:

A quote I may use:

5. The unreal is more powerful than the real, because nothing is as perfect as you can imagine it because its only intangible ideas, concepts, beliefs, fantasies that last. Stone crumbles. Wood rots. People, well, they die. But things as fragile as athought, a dream, a legend, they can go on and on.

- Chuck Palahnuik

Assignment: What is your view of the idea that the unreal such as concepts,and ideas is more powerful than the real such as stones and wood? Plan and writean essay in which you develop your point of view on this issue. Support your position with reasoning and examples taken from your reading, studies, experience, or observations.

Issue:

_____

_____

My position:

_____

_____

Example 1:

_____

_____

Source:

_____

Example 2:

_____

_____

Source:

_____

Example 3:

_____

_____

Source:

_____

A quote I may use:

_____

6. The notion that journalists should strive to remain objective has been challenged in recent years as new reporting styles have come into vogue. For instance, a novel style of journalism, known as "gonzo journalism", emerged in the1970s. This form, which remains popular today, is characterized by a punchy style, rough and occasionally sarcastic language, and an apparent disregard for conventional journalistic writing customs. Unlike traditional journalist, gonzojournalists use the power of both emotions and personal experience to convey their messages.

Assignment: Is writing subjectively on a story better than adhering to the objectivity prized in standard journalistic writing? Plan and write an essay in which you develop your point of view on this issue. Support your position with reasoning and examples taken from your reading, studies, experience, or observations.

Issue:

_____

My position:

_____

Example 1:

_____

Source:

_____

Example 2:

_____

Source:

_____

Example 3:

_____

_____

Source:

_____

A quote I may use:

_____

_____

7. Since the advent of television, social commentators have been evaluating its rolein a modern society. "Television makes you stupid." Virtually all current theories ofthe medium come down to this simple statement.

Assignment: What is your view of the idea that watching television undermines the viewers' ability to perceive? Plan and write an essay in which you develop your point of view on this issue. Support your position with reasoning and examples taken from your reading, studies, experience, or observations.

Issue:

_____

_____

My position:

_____

_____

Example 1:

_____

_____

Source:

_____

Example 2:

_____

Source:

_____

Example 3:

_____

Source:

_____

A quote I may use:

_____

8. Soon silence will have passed into legend. Man has turned his back on silence. Day after day he invents machines and devices that increase noise and distract humanity from the essence of life, contemplation, meditation... tooting, howling, screeching, booming, crashing, whistling, grinding, and trilling bolster hisego. His anxiety subsides. His inhuman void spreads monstrously like a gray vegetation.

- Jean Arp

Assignment: What is your view of the idea that technology distracts humanity from the essence of life? Plan and write an essay in which you develop your point of view on this issue. Support your position with reasoning and examples taken from your reading, studies, experience, or observations.

Issue:

_____

My position:

_____

Example 1:

_____

Source:

_____

Example 2:

_____

Source:

_____

Example 3:

_____

Source:

_____

A quote I may use:

_____

9. Our destiny changes with our thought; we shall become what we wish to become, do what we wish to do, when our habitual thought corresponds

with our desire.

- Orison Swett Mardon

Assignment: Do you think people control their own destiny or their destiny are controlled by others? Plan and write an essay in which you develop your point of view on this issue. Support your position with reasoning and examples taken from your reading, studies, experience, or observations.

Issue:

_____

_____

My position:

_____

_____

Example 1:

_____

_____

Source:

_____

Example 2:

_____

_____

Source:

_____

Example 3:

_____

_____

Source:

_____

A quote I may use:

_____

Answers and Explanations

1. Issue: It is better to forgive than to revenge in one's life.

My position: You have to decide if you agree or disagree with issue as stated. In other words, do you agree that it is better to forgive than to revenge in one's life or do you believe it is better to revenge than to forgive in one's life? It seems as though you should agree with issue, or you would have to make a very good example to support your position.

(Examples for the position that forgiveness is better than revenge are as follows)

Example 1: Dr. Robert Enright from the University of Wisconsin-Madison founded the International Forgiveness Institute and is considered the initiator of forgiveness studies. He developed a 20-Step Process Model of Forgiveness. Recent work has focused on what kind of person is more likely to be forgiving. The first study to look at how forgiveness improves physical health discovered that when people think about forgiving an offender, it leads to improved functioning in their cardiovascular and nervous systems. Another study at the University of Wisconsin found the more forgiving people were, the less they suffered from a wide range of illnesses. The less forgiving people reported a greater number of health problems. So many studies show that people who forgive are happier and healthier than those who hold resentments.

Source: scientific research

Example 2: Many people in India were at first against Mother Teresa, and made offensive statements at her but she still forgave each and every one of them and she won respect finally from them. So forgiving someone will not change the past but will improve the communication standard between the two in future. It is a hard sacrificing decision but end result will be relieving. Forgiveness eases up the situation and makes individuals think positive of the other person, not forgetting what they have done but just to forgive and move on with life.

Source: philanthropist

Example 3: Another good one is Nelson Mandela. He fought against the racist system of apartheid in South Africa and was imprisoned for 27 years. When he wasr eleased, he harbored no ill will and became South Africa's president in 1994. His forgiveness helped South Africa transition from rule by whites only to a true democratic system. Afterwards, the Truth and Reconciliation Committee was set up to uncover the facts of South African apartheid and to forgive those involved.

Desmond Tutu, who presided over the commission, wrote a book about it called "No Future Without Forgiveness" .

Source: politician

A quote I may use:

The weak can never forgive. Forgiveness is the attribute of the strong.

- Mahatma Gandhi

2. Issue: Online social networking is changing the real meaning of friendship.

My position: Do you think online social networking is changing the real meaning offriendship? Or do you believe that online social networking is not changing the real meaning of friendship?

(Examples for the position that social networking is not changing the real meaning of friendship)

Example 1: An online survey has revealed that face-to-face encounters are, perhaps unsurprisingly, still the most important factor in close friendships. Some 90 per cent of the online friends rated as "close" have been met face-to-face, with the remaining 10 per cent likely to be friends of close friends, perceived as having many of the mutual friend's attributes and therefore "low risk" .

Source: online survey

Example 2: Psychology studies show that it is easier to spot honest signals when meeting someone face-to-face using facial and bodily cues where as it is harder to spot dishonest signals online. So the importance of honest signals is a fundamental concept in behavioral ecology.

Source: psychological studies

Example 3: A female song bird invests in a mate based on the quality of his voice, as this is an honest signal indicating the fitness of the bird. In the same way, people choose friends based on their "quality" , and this can only be assessed when there are honest signals being given.

Source: science

A quote I may use:

Friendship is a pretty full-time occupation if you really are friendly with somebody.

You cannot have too many friends because then you're just not really friends.

- Truman Capote

3. Issue: Human society in its progress toward the clichéd "global village" is liable to make the world less stable not more stable.

My position: Do you think human society in its progress toward the clichéd "global village" is liable to make the world less stable not more stable? Or do you believe that human society in its progress toward the clichéd "global village" is liable to make the world table more stable?

(Examples for the position that human society in its progress toward the clichéd "global village" is liable to make the world less stable not more stable)

Example 1: If we traveled 10,000 miles from home only to find no new people, no new places, no new styles of living, just a copy of what we experienced back home, how infinitely poorer we would be.

Source: observations

Example 2: A rainforest ecosystem community is directly related to species diversity.

The more complex the structure, the greater its species diversity is. A rainforest is a system that supports interacting units including trees, soil, insects, animals and man.

So the diversity is important to stability in the natural world.

Source: ecology

Example 3: There are about $171,000$ words in the language of English, according to the second edition of the 20-volume Oxford English Dictionary. Over half of these words are nouns, about a quarter adjectives, and about a seventh verbs; the rest is made up of exclamations, conjunctions, prepositions, suffixes, etc. So if there were not diversity in language, could we have the chance to read Shakespeare's beautiful sonnets?

Source: literature and linguistics

A quote I may use:

There never were in the world two opinions alike, no more than two hairs or two grains; the most universal quality is diversity.

- Michel de Montaigne

4. Issue: Human being's highest happiness lies in seeking pleasure.

My position: Do you think human being's highest happiness lie in seeking pleasure?

Or do you believe that human being's highest happiness lie in hard work? It seems as though you should disagree with issue by picking the side that human being's highest happiness lie in hard work, or you should find a very good example to support you position.

(Examples for the position that human being's highest happiness lies in hard work)

Example 1: According to Dr. Sonja Lyubomirsky, University of California Riverside, the pursuit of happiness has many benefits.

1. Higher income and superior work outcomes; better quality work

2. Larger social rewards such as longer marriages, more friends

3. More activity and energy

4. Better physical health; lower stress and less pain

5. Longer life

The benefits of happiness describe what most of us feel is an ideal life⋯ more fun at work, many friends, successful relationships, lots of energy, and long life with less pain. And that's not all! Dr. Sonja's asks that "if happiness is so beneficial, and we all seem to be obsessed with the notion, why aren't more of us happy?" The study suggests that human beings' focus may be misplaced: "Pleasure-seeking, quick fixes, and self-gratification are proven to have limited long-term effects on true happiness." It is not smiling on the outside when you are really churning on the inside. Real happiness has more to do with effort than attitude. In her study, she found that the secret to happiness is hard work not "quick-fixes" , and "compulsive self-gratification" . She said, "Effort and hard work offer the most promising route to happiness⋯engagement in activities that promote one's highest potential⋯"

Source: research and study

Example 2: Edison is considered one of the most prolific inventors in history, holding 1,093 US patents in his name, as well as many patents in the United Kingdom, France, and Germany. He is credited with numerous inventions that contributed tomass communication and, in particular, telecommunications. These included a stock ticker, a mechanical vote recorder, a battery for an electric car, electrical power, recorded music and motion pictures. His hard and advanced work in these fields was an out growth of his early career as a telegraph operator, not to mention the inventionof the long-lasting, practical electric light bulb. His development of many devices that greatly influenced life around the world results from his hard work. He said, "Hardwork is where my great happiness comes from."

Source: scientist

Example 3: The movie "The Pursuit of Happiness" is a 2006 American biographical drama film and based on the life of Chris Gardner who was an on-and-off-homeless sales-turned stockbroker through hard work. In 1981, in San Francisco, Chris Gardner invests his family's savings in Osteo National bone-density scanners, a portable medical imaging device, which proves to be a white elephant and financially breaks the family and as a result, his wife Linda leaves him and their son Christopher.Chris is barely able to make ends meet and later he is unable to make his rent and is evicted from his apartment. Homeless, he is forced at one point to stay in a bathroom at a BART station. One day, he meets a manager for Dean Witter and impresses him by solving a Rubiks Cube during a short cab ride. This new relationship earns him the chance to interview for a stockbroker internship which he is offered, but nearly turns down when the position turns out to be unpaid. Disadvantaged by his limited work hours, and knowing that maximizing his client contacts and profits is the only way toearn the one position that he and his 19 competitors are fighting for, Chris works very hard and develops a number of ways to work more efficiently and reaches out to potential high value customers defying protocol. Despite his personal challenges, he never reveals his circumstances to his co-workers even going so far as to loan one of his bosses five dollars for a cab, a sum he can barely afford. At the end, Chris is called into a meeting with his managers. His struggle has paid off and he is offered the position. As Chris said, happiness doesn't depend on who you are and what you have, it depends mainly on your hard work.

Source: movie

A quote I may use:

Happiness lies in being privileged to work hard for long hours in doing whatever you think is worth doing. Note the individual and subjective nature of each case. No two are alike and there is no reason to expect them to be. Each man or woman must find for himself or herself that occupation in which hard work and long hours make him or her happy. Contrariwise, if you are looking for shorter hours and longer vacations and early retirement, you are in the wrong job. Perhaps you need to take up bank robbing, or peeking in a sideshow, or even politics.

- Robert Heinlein

5. Issue: The unreal such as concepts and ideas is more powerful than the real such as stones and wood.

My position: Do you agree that the unreal is more powerful than the real? Or do you believe that the real is actually more powerful than the unreal?

(Examples for the position that the real is more powerful than the unreal are as follows)

Example 1: Some concepts and ideas, no matter how valuable and how powerful they are, are given by philosophers or thinkers or ordinary people who are humanbeings. Confucius' philosophy emphasized personal and governmental morality, correctness of social relationships, justice and sincerity, and he has gained wide acceptance around the world. He died about $2,000$ years ago, but undoubtedly, he is still considered one of the most powerful thinkers today. Those famous powerful teachings which has been popular for thousands of years such as "A superior man is modest in his speech, but exceeds in his actions" , "Better a diamond with a flaw than a pebble without" and "Choose a job you love, and you will never have to work a day in your life" come from nowhere but a man named Confucius. Or we may say the unreal originates from the real.

Source: philosopher

There are many of examples of other stories of philosophers that you could.

Example 2: Although best remembered as prime minister of England during World War II, Churchill was also an accomplished historian, having published dozens of volumes on the history of England and Europe. Additionally, he has been noted as a master of oratory. Churchill was awarded the Nobel Prize for Literature in 1953 "for his historical and biographical presentations and for the scintillating oratory in which he has stood forth as a defender of human values." There is no denying of the role that Churchill has played in World War II and what his sayings such as "A pessimist sees the difficulty in every opportunity; an optimist sees the opportunity in every difficulty" and "All the great things are simple, and many can be expressed in a single word: freedom, justice, honor, duty, mercy, hope" have inspired and influenced people. So whenever we say how powerful some ideas are, there is one thing we can not ignore that they are from people who have abilities to create powerful concepts.

Source: politician and historian

Example 3: When Ed. Roberts coined the term "personal computer" and introduced the Altair 8800 in 1975, he would probably never think of how popular and how powerful a personal computer would be in fifteen years or so. He of course put a lot of thoughts and ideas and efforts in the process of designing such a real thing.

However, the real thing, computer, has more potential power than what a creator' sidea could reach.

Source: science

A quote I may use:

Lead me from the unreal to the Real.

Lead me from darkness to Light.

Lead me from death to Immortality.

- Sri Chinmoy

6. Issue: Writing subjectively on a story is better than adhering to the objectivity prized in standard journalistic writing.

My position: Do you agree that writing subjectively on a story is better than adhering to the objectivity prized in standard journalistic writing? Or do you agree that adhering to the objectivity prized in standard journalistic writing is better than writing subjectively on a story?

(Examples for the position that adhering to the objectivity prized in standard journalistic writing is better than presenting an unedited perspective on a story are as follows)

Example 1: What if it would a report on the World War II. Would readers need to see the facts about what were really happening there or would they have to read as tory, which was written in a subjective way, saying probably what the Nazi did was right if the gonzo journalist were on the side of Nazi. Readers need simply the facts not the fictions.

Source: studies

Example 2: Fact checking and accuracy are valued journalistic traits.

Throughout the nineteenth century, the process by which news was delivered to a consuming public had strong parallels in the ancient art of storytelling. But in the mid-1860's, the seeds of destruction of the genre had been planted with the invention of the inverted pyramid. The adoption of the inverted pyramid, no matter whose version of its invention one may accept, was based on the concept that the most important aspect of news delivery was tied to facts and that somehow or other these facts were not tainted with personal agenda.

Source: observations

Example 3: Objectivity is not only a trait for journalists but also applies to many other professionals in many other fields such as accountants and translators and interpreters.

Source: observations

A quote I may use:

As a scientist, objectivity is one of my most deeply held values. If we could just try harder, I once thought, surely we could each see the world as others see it and learn to respect one another's views more readily. But I learned from the Pirahas, our expectations, our culture, and our experiences can render even perceptions of the environment nearly incommensurable cross-culturally.

- Daniel Everett

7. Issue: Watching television undermines the viewers' ability to perceive.

My position: Do you agree that watching television undermines the viewers' ability to perceive? Or do you believe that watching television doesn't undermine the viewers' ability to perceive?

(Examples for the position that watching television undermines the viewers' ability to perceive are as follows)

Example 1: One of Britain's most respected directors, Ken Loach, said at the London film festival in 2010 that highly paid, time-serving television executives are killing creativity and making the medium one big "grotesque reality game" . The director, who first joined the BBC 47 years ago and made plays such as Cathy

Come Home, launched an excoriating attack on the culture of television today. He also said that "Television has now become the enemy of creativity. Television kills creativity."

Source: media

Example 2: Some may argue that television is the window to the world and watching TV programs which are informative and absorbing is worth it. Channels like Discovery, History, and National Geographic can be of highly educational value. But the question is comparing to the people who watch soaps, sitcoms, reality shows, dramas and cop shows, how many people are there watching informative programs.

Source: observation

Example 3: Television is also awful, and kids watch so much of it. It's not surprising that there's been much sociological research on its effects. Recent study also shows that kids who watch a lot of TV not only tend to be more aggressive but violent. What's even worse, the studies indicate that kids with lower IQ scores also tend to watch more TV.

Source: research

A quote I may use:

The perceptive act is a reaction of the mind upon the object of which it is the perception.

- Samuel Alexander

8. Issue: Technology distracts humanity from the essence of life.

My position: Do you agree that technology distracts humanity from the essence of life? Or do you believe that technology doesn't distract humanity from the essence of life?

(Examples for the position that technology distracts humanity from the essence of life are as follows)

Example 1: Since man started using tools, technology has shaped human society. Stone tools opened up new sources of food, enabling primitive man to expand in population. These tools also changed the social structure of primitive man, putting more emphasis on males to capture large game. Social division of labor caused by technology changes hence made the society a male-domination one. Sex discrimination against women occurred.

Source: history

Example 2: Cell phones, copiers, emails and fax machines are the basis for our daily life. People tend to be more attentive to transmit information quickly and cheaply. They ignore the "price" that modern technologies cost to human beings. We often notice that people spend lunch hour texting messages to someone else by the phone instead of their friends sitting next to them.

Source: experience

Example 3: Many college students have the experience that some students, instead of turning off their cell phones for the duration of the class, leave the classroom to take calls without slightest hint of embarrassment.

Source: experience

A quote I may use:

It is appallingly obvious our technology has exceeded our humanity.

- Albert Einstein

9. Issue: People control their own destiny.

My position: Do you agree that people control their own destiny? Or do you believe that people's destiny is controlled by others?

(Examples for the position that people control their own destiny are as follows)

Example 1: The play Antigone, written by Sophocles, expresses viewpoints of the author in regards to several issues. One such issue is that of destiny. The play's events reveal that Sophocles believes that all people control their own fate based upon the actions they take. He does not deem that all people have predetermined paths of life. The actions that Antigone take throughout the play unmistakably identify Sophocles belief that people control their own destiny. She causes her own collapse and death. Her first mistake was her decision to violate Creon's rule by burying Polyneices. She makes this choice even though she knows that the penalty for burying Polyneices is death. With this knowledge she persists and puts herself in a risky situation. Her stubbornness plays a major role in her death as well.

Source: literature

Example 2: Locus of control is the perceived way an individual attributes behavior. The factors involved are labeled "external and internal" control. Internal locus of control refers to the perception of positive or negative events as being a consequence of one's own actions and under one's own control. People with internal locus of control believe they control their own destiny, and they are more likely to work for achievements, and raise their behavior goals when the first is succeeded.

Source: psychology

Example 3: Euthanasia, a painless and easy death according to the explanation of Webster's Dictionary, is a very sensitive and debatable topic in today's society. Currently, many moral and ethical arguments are against this method since it is still a strong belief that man has right to privacy, and control over his body and destiny. That's also why using euthanasia is still considered illegal.

Source: medicine

A quote I may use:

The best years of your life are the ones in which you decide your problems are your own. You do not blame them on your mother, the ecology, or the president. You realize that you control your own destiny.

- Albert Ellis

Step two: Find examples
-two examples are fine, too

Time: 2 minutes

According to the College Board, the essays prompt "give students the opportunity to use a broad range of experiences, learning, and ideas to support their points of view on the issue addressed. Because the prompt requires students to address a specific issue, students will not be able to prepare an essay in advance that will effectively address the essay assignment."

Yes, you will not be able to prepare a specific essay over a particular topic in advance. However, you can and should thoroughly prepare the examples that will earn you a top score on your SAT, with the help of the summary of example source, remember?

Before you go into the exam room, review your example source summary first and try to remember at least ten examples from different category. On the test day pick the best two or three examples which are your strongest arguments, or the ones from the best sources. But try to vary the examples, as we said in the writing tips.

Some students wonder how many examples they should include into their essays. Would it be two or three?

A student in my class said he felt like he can write better with two examples in two body paragraphs because he had more could have more time to elaborate on his ideas to be more convincing but he doubted if using only two examples penalize his score.

The answer would be "quality over quantity" . Many test takers scored high although they gave only two examples. But the fact is if your examples you cited support your position or not and how strongly and powerfully they are used.

Step three: Write introductory paragraph
-state your position

Time: 2 minutes

Now start your essay with an introductory paragraph. This opening paragraph is important because it provides a quick description regarding the most critical facts to be discussed in relation to the SAT questions being asked. It must get straight to the point, dealing directly with the topics involved and not flander around the topic in anyway. In fact, the first initial five words are most vital because these are the ones that stick in the mind of the SAT grader immediately. Ultimately, the introduction will entice any SAT grader to continue reading the rest of the SAT essay.

It also has been an open secret in the SAT industry that essay graders spent most of their time poring over the opening and closing paragraphs. Because there are so many essays to grade and so little time to grade them, many SAT graders literally skim over the body portion. They focus on the opening and closing because those are the paragraphs that best indicate whether you actually answered the question posed.

So make sure this paragraph, which, I suggest, consists of three to five sentences, clearly introduces the SAT question and your position, and if possible, how you are going to support your position. Most importantly it catches the interest of the graders, encouraging them to read the remainder of your essay.

Step four: Begin the body
-use examples to support your position

Time: 15 minutes

The body is your content and should support your position made in your opening. Try to give two or three reasons for why you have taken the position you did on the prompt question. If you can only come up with one reason, give a detailed explanation of why it supports your stand, and say why it is important enough to make the case on its own.

For the reasons, I also mean examples. In life, you can tell people you don't like something or somebody. But you need evidence, or powerful examples to support your statement. Otherwise, no one would be convinced and no one would listen to you. For SAT essay, it's the same case. Use examples to support your position and they have to be strong and powerful.

In detail, the example must be directly relevant to your position. In our case, if the example did not directly support that people are driven by greed and recognition, it should not be included in your response.

You must be able to fully develop the example by explaining details such as names, relevant facts, time period, sources, etc.

Meanwhile, be direct and to the point. Don't get wordy or you will get stuck in these paragraphs.

The body is usually composed of three paragraphs and each body paragraph should be from four to six sentences long, and if possible, start each body paragraph with a topic sentence that explains what the paragraph is about and how it relates to your position. But this is not a must. Students do have different styles of writing. Just make sure if you don't have a special opening in the body paragraph and don't know what to write, follow this rule.

One more thing, I hate to say, but it's a fact that the more scholarly your examples are, the better your score will be and the strongest, most impressive examples tend to come from history and literature. You can use your own personal experience but don't rely on them unless the SAT essay prompt closely relates to your personal experience.

Step five: Write the conclusion
-you must close

Time: 1 minute

If you get caught up in the writing of your essay and you don't close you will pay dearly. You must close! The introduction paragraph and the closing paragraph are the two most important parts of your essay. Leave either one of them out and you will receive a low score even if your message is awesome.

Gracefully exit your essay by making a quick wrap-up sentence, and then end on some memorable thought, perhaps a quotation, or an interesting twist of logic, or some call to action. Remember the closing can be the difference between a good score and a great score.

Step six: Show variety in sentence structure

To make your writing more interesting, you should try to vary your sentences in terms of length and structure. You can make some of your sentences long and others short.

Adding sentence variety to prose can give it life and rhythm. Too many sentences with the same structure and length can grow monotonous for readers. Varying sentence style and structure can also reduce repetition and add emphasis. Long sentences work well for incorporating a lot of information, and short sentences can often maximize crucial points. These general tips may help add variety to similar sentences.

1. Vary the rhythm by alternating short and long sentences.

Example: The most interesting person I know is Winston Smith. He started his own business twenty years ago. He now has a fleet of 50-distance trucks. He never forgot how hard it was to get his first loan to start his business. He started a program to help enterprising college graduates who want to start their own business.

Revision: The most interesting person I know is Winston Smith. He started his own business twenty years ago and now owns 50-distance trucks. Mr. Smith has never forgotten how hard it was to get his first loan. As a result, he started a program to help enterprising college graduates who want to start their own business.

2. Vary sentence openings.

If too many sentences start with the same word, especially "The" , "It" , "This" , or "I" , they can grow tedious for readers, so changing opening words and phrases can be refreshing. Below are alternative openings for a fairly standard sentence. Notice that different beginnings can alter not only the structure but also the emphasis of the sentence.

Example: The biggest coincidence that day happened when David and I ended up sitting next to each other at the Roland Garros.

Possible Revisions:

▶ Coincidentally, Charles and I ended up sitting right next to each other at Roland Garros.

▶ In an amazing coincidence, Charles and I ended up sitting next to each other at Roland Garros.

▶ Sitting next to Charles at Roland Garros was a tremendous coincidence.

▶ But the biggest coincidence that day happened when Charles and I ended up sitting next to each other at Roland Garros.

▶ When I SAT down at Roland Garros, I realized that, by sheer coincidence, I was directly next to Charles.

▶ Though I hadn't made any advance arrangements with Charles, we ended up sitting right next to each other at Roland Garros.

▶ Many amazing coincidences occurred that day, but nothing topped sitting right next to Charles at Roland Garros.

Step seven: Diversity in word choice

For the diversity of word choice, try to practice the following list.

argue: contend basic: fundamental

cause: engender, elicit

caring: altruistic

common: prevalent, conventional

different: discrepant, diverse

difficult: problematic

difficulty: dilemma, quagmire

easy: viable, tenable

emphasize: underscore

false: fallacious

hard: vexing

illustrate: highlight, exemplify, epitomize

important: unparalleled, unprecedented

impossible: implausible

natural: inherent, innate, intrinsic

necessary: implicit, underlying

new: novel

obviously: ostensibly

part: aspect

possible: plausible

quite: particularly, exceptionally

result: outcome, aftermath

selfish: egoistical

Step eight: Check and polish
-revise for grammatical and writing faults

Time: 1 minute

You're not done writing your essay until you've polished your language by correcting the grammar, making sentences flow, incorporating rhythm, emphasis, adjusting the formality, giving it a level-headed tone, and making other intuitive edits. Proofread until it reads just how you want it to sound. But if you don't have time, take it easy, minor slips in grammar or spelling are not likely to hurt your SAT essay score. However, a pattern of mistakes might suggest that you just aren't competent in standard written English.

Also ensure that you state each of your point clearly and succinctly in each topic sentence. Customize each of your topic sentences to reflect your essay's thesis. Then elaborate on the topic sentence in your respective body paragraph. Check the conclusion to see if you end your essay with a thoughtful line to stand out to the reader.

Check your handwriting as well. Graders aren't supposed to mark essays down for bad penmanship, but if they honestly can't make out what you've written, you may get a lower score than you deserve.

S.A.T Chapter IV

Writing Essays Practice

　　如何合理分配時間，確保自己在二十五分鐘內完成命題作文是困擾很多學生的一個問題。本章為考生提供了七道 SAT 標準作文試題，並對寫作步驟——審題、搜索例證、文章架構、正式寫作和修正——進行詳細分解。練習並熟悉這些寫作步驟，可以說明你有效分配和利用時間。考試當天，自然會得心應手。同時，本章還為考生提供了評分標準圖表。你可以在完成作文寫作後，進行自我評估，分析自己的寫作弱點，比如得分低是因為句子結構單調，用詞不準確，還是文章缺乏調理，論據沒有說服力。然後，有針對性地閱讀上一章寫作技巧部分，對作文做出修改。

To help you apply the strategy that you've learned in the previous chapter for writing a great SAT essay in 25 minutes, the answer sheets for the practice essays list a predetermined timing guide after each essay prompt. Use it as you write your essays. It will help you manage your time and pace yourself. The worksheets direct you through the step-by-step process for planning, organizing, and writing your essay. The practice is aimed to help you become familiar with the procedures so that all the steps about writing an essay will just come naturally to you on the test day.

How to use the practice essays

　　1. Plan and write each essay based on the process given.

2. Use the self-evaluation chart to rate your essay and score yourself.

3. According to the chart, where could you do better? Is it grammar, word choice or organization? Read chapter two to see how you might enhance your performance in your essay.

4. Revise your essay.

5. Evaluate your revised essay. How is your performance this time? What is the difference? State to yourself how your revised essay is better than the first one.

Practice Essay 1

Directions: Consider carefully the following statement and the assignment below it. Then plan and write an essay that explains your ideas as persuasively as possible. Keep in mind that the support you provide—both reasons and examples—will help make your view convincing to the reader.

> Over the past 10 years, there has been accelerated use of cellular or mobile phones. In the United States alone, there are an estimated 167 million cell phone subscribers (Cellular Telecommunications Industry Association, 2004). Don Cheadle, as Graham, in Crash, said, "It's the sense of touch. In any real city, you walk, you know? You brush past people, people bump into you. In L.A., nobody touches you. We're always behind this metal and glass. I think we miss that touch so much, that we crash into each other, just so we can feel something."

Assignment: Do cell phones bring people closer or farther apart? Plan and write an essay in which you develop your point of view on this issue. Support your position with reasoning and examples taken from your reading, studies, experience, or observations.

Follow the steps while writing your essay.

Step 1: Read the prompt carefully and decide your position. (3 minutes)

Decide whether you agree or disagree. you must respond to the assigned topic; you must choose yes or no.

_____

_____

_____

_____

Step 2: Brainstorm your ideas and write the examples you might use in the space below. (2 minutes)

Vary the examples: pick examples from different category

_____

_____

_____

_____

Step 3: Write introductory paragraph. (2 minutes)

Do not wander around the topic: clearly introduces the SAT question and your position. Try to catch the interest of the readers.

_____

_____

_____

_____

Step 4: Begin the body. (15 minutes)

Be sure to include at least two examples and it is usually composed of three paragraphs.

Body paragraph 1

_____

_____

_____

Body paragraph 2

_____

_____

_____

Body paragraph 3

_____

_____

_____

Step 5: Write the conclusion.(1 minute)

Repetition can be annoying. Gracefully exit your essay by making a quick wrap-up sentence, and then end on some memorable thought, perhaps a quotation, or an interesting twist of logic, or some call to action.

_____

_____

_____

Step 6: Check and polish.(1 minute)

Gracefully exit your essay by making a quick wrap-up sentence, and then end on some memorable thought, perhaps a quotation, or an interesting twist of logic, or some call to action.

▶ cross out the redundancies.

▶ smooth out any irrelevant words.

▶ check your grammar.

Self-evaluation Chart

	Overall impression	Organization and development	Thesis and examples
6	develops effectively and insightfully a point of view on the issue and demonstrates strong critical thinking; outstanding writing competence; using appropriate examples, reasons to support its position	well organized and thoroughly developed; clearly focused and coherent	demonstrates excellent perception and clarity; original; includes apt and specific facts, examples or references
5	develops effectively a point of view on the issue and demonstrates strong critical thinking; good writing competence; use appropriate examples, reasons to support its position; less incisive and insightful than the highest-scoring essay	well organized and focused; demonstrates coherence and progression of ideas	demonstrates good perception and clarity; includes specific facts, examples or references
4	demonstrates adequate critical thinking; competent writing; includes references and examples	generally organized and focused, demonstrating some coherence and progression of ideas	perceptive and clear; includes facts, examples or references
3	develops a point of view on the issue; exhibits some critical thinking, but may do so inconsistently or use inadequate examples	limited in its organization or focus, or may demonstrate some lapses in coherence or progression of ideas	somewhat clear but with incomplete or confusing thinking

	Overall impression	Organization and development	Thesis and examples
2	develops a point of view on the issue that is vague or seriously limited; demonstrates weak critical thinking; provides inappropriate examples to support its position	poorly organized and/or focused, or demonstrates serious problems with coherence or development of ideas; fail to respond to the issue	very little clarity; irrelevant examples
1	develops no viable point of view on the issue; provides little or no evidence to support its position	disorganized or unfocused	very irrelevant statement or off the topic

	Sentence structure	Word choice	Grammar
6	demonstrates meaningful variety in sentence structure	exhibits skillful use of language, using a varied, accurate and apt vocabulary	virtually error free
5	demonstrates variety in sentence structure	exhibits facility in the use of language, using appropriate vocabulary; a few errors	occasional minor errors
4	demonstrates some variety in sentence structure	exhibits adequate but inconsistent facility in the use of language, using generally appropriate vocabulary	some minor errors
3	lacks variety or demonstrates problems in sentence structure	displays developing facility in the use of language, but sometimes uses weak vocabulary	some major errors
2	little or no variation; some frequent problems in sentence structure	use very limited vocabulary or incorrect word choice	some severe errors

	Sentence structure	Word choice	Grammar
1	demonstrates severe problems in sentence structure	displays numerous errors in vocabulary	contains pervasive errors

How to score your essays: Evaluate your essay in each of the area on the chart. Enter the numbers on the lines below. Then calculate the average of the six numbers to get your score. On the SAT, at least two graders will mark your essay on a scale of 1 to 6, with 6 being the highest. So you may ask a friend or teacher to rate your essay to get your final score.

Self-evaluation (Each area is rated 6 to 1)

Overall impression   _____

Organization and development   _____

Thesis and examples   _____

Sentence structure   _____

Word choice   _____

Grammar   _____

Total   _____

Divide by 6 for your score   _____

Evaluation from a friend or teacher (Each area is rated 6 to 1)

Overall impression   _____

Organization and development   _____

Thesis and examples   _____

Sentence structure   _____

Word choice   _____

Grammar   _____

Total   _____

Divide by 6 for your score   _____

Practice Essay 2

Directions: Consider carefully the following statement and the assignment below it. Then plan and write an essay that explains your ideas as persuasively as possible. Keep in mind that the support you provide - both reasons and examples - will help make your view convincing to the reader.

> Freedom and happiness is the yearning of every human being's heart. It is the quest of the human spirit. From the beginning of time, man has always searched for these tenets of life. It is as if the seed of freedom is planted in the heart and soul. Every adventure of man has been the expression of this freedom; it has been the desire for, or the expression of his state of happiness. Freedom and happiness is what you are truly looking for. Every other thing that you have ever sought to acquire or achieve is your means of achieving the state of freedom and happiness.
>
> - Christopher Kabamba

Assignment: What is your view of the idea that desire for achievement and quest for material possessions is the need for the expression of freedom and experiencing of true happiness? Plan and write an essay in which you develop your point of view on this issue. Support your position with reasoning and examples taken from your reading, studies, experience, or observations.

Follow the steps while writing your essay.

Step 1: Read the prompt carefully and decide your position.(3 minutes)

Decide whether you agree or disagree. you must respond to the assigned topic; you must choose yes or no.

_____

_____

_____

Step 2: Brainstorm your ideas and write the examples you might use in

the space below. (2 minutes)

Vary the examples: pick examples from different category

_____

_____

_____

_____

Step 3: Write introductory paragraph.(2 minutes)

Do not wander around the topic: clearly introduces the SAT question and your position. Try to catch the interest of the readers.

_____

_____

_____

_____

Step 4: Begin the body.(15 minutes)

Be sure to include at least two examples and it is usually composed of three paragraphs.

Body paragraph 1

_____

_____

_____

_____

Body paragraph 2

_____

_____

_____

Body paragraph 3

_____

_____

_____

_____

Step 5: Write the conclusion.(1 minute)

Repetition can be annoying. Gracefully exit your essay by making a quick wrap-up sentence, and then end on some memorable thought, perhaps a quotation, or an interesting twist of logic, or some call to action.

_____

_____

_____

Step 6: Check and polish.(1 minute)

Gracefully exit your essay by making a quick wrap-up sentence, and then end on some memorable thought, perhaps a quotation, or an interesting twist of logic, or some call to action.

► cross out the redundancies.

► smooth out any irrelevant words.

► check your grammar.

Practice Essay 3

Directions: Consider carefully the following statement and the assignment below it. Then plan and write an essay that explains your ideas as persuasively as possible. Keep in mind that the support you provide-both reasons and examples-will help make your view convincing to the reader.

All of the biggest technological inventions created by man-the airplane, the automobile, the computer-says little about his intelligence, but speaks volumes about his laziness.

- Mark Kennedy

Assignment: What is your view of idea that technology has made people lazy? Plan and write an essay in which you develop your point of view on this issue. Support your position with reasoning and examples taken from your reading, studies, experience, or observations.

Follow the steps while writing your essay.

Step 1: Read the prompt carefully and decide your position.(3 minutes)

Decide whether you agree or disagree. you must respond to the assigned topic; you must choose yes or no.

_____

_____

_____

_____

Step 2: Brainstorm your ideas and write the examples you might use in the space below. (2 minutes)

Vary the examples: pick examples from different category

_____

_____

_____

_____

Step 3: Write introductory paragraph.(2 minutes)

Do not wander around the topic: clearly introduces the SAT question and your position. Try to catch the interest of the readers.

_____

_____

_____

Step 4: Begin the body.(15 minutes)

Be sure to include at least two examples and it is usually composed of three paragraphs.

Body paragraph 1

Body paragraph 2

Body paragraph 3

Step 5: Write the conclusion.(1 minute)

Repetition can be annoying. Gracefully exit your essay by making a quick wrap-up sentence, and then end on some memorable thought, perhaps a quotation, or an interesting twist of logic, or some call to action.

Step 6: Check and polish.(1 minute)

Gracefully exit your essay by making a quick wrap-up sentence, and then end on some memorable thought, perhaps a quotation, or an interesting twist of logic, or some call to action.

Self-evaluation Chart

	Overall impression	Organization and development	Thesis and examples
6	develops effectively and insightfully a point of view on the issue and demonstrates strong critical thinking; outstanding writing competence; using appropriate examples, reasons to support its position	well organized and thoroughly developed; clearly focused and coherent	demonstrates excellent perception and clarity; original; includes apt and specific facts, examples or references
5	develops effectively a point of view on the issue and demonstrates strong critical thinking; good writing competence; use appropriate examples, reasons to support its position; less incisive and insightful than the highest-scoring essay	well organized and focused; demonstrates coherence and progression of ideas	demonstrates good perception and clarity; includes specific facts, examples or references
4	demonstrates adequate critical thinking; competent writing; includes references and examples	generally organized and focused, demonstrating some coherence and progression of ideas	perceptive and clear; includes facts, examples or references
3	develops a point of view on the issue; exhibits some critical thinking, but may do so inconsistently or use inadequate examples	limited in its organization or focus, or may demonstrate some lapses in coherence or progression of ideas	somewhat clear but with incomplete or confusing thinking

	Overall impression	Organization and development	Thesis and examples
2	develops a point of view on the issue that is vague or seriously limited; demonstrates weak critical thinking; provides inappropriate examples to support its position	poorly organized and/or focused, or demonstrates serious problems with coherence or development of ideas; fail to respond to the issue	very little clarity; irrelevant examples
1	develops no viable point of view on the issue; provides little or no evidence to support its position	disorganized or unfocused	very irrelevant statement or off the topic

	Sentence structure	Word choice	Grammar
6	demonstrates meaningful variety in sentence structure	exhibits skillful use of language, using a varied, accurate and apt vocabulary	virtually error free
5	demonstrates variety in sentence structure	exhibits facility in the use of language, using appropriate vocabulary; a few errors	occasional minor errors
4	demonstrates some variety in sentence structure	exhibits adequate but inconsistent facility in the use of language, using generally appropriate vocabulary	some minor errors
3	lacks variety or demonstrates problems in sentence structure	displays developing facility in the use of language, but sometimes uses weak vocabulary	some major errors

	Sentence structure	Word choice	Grammar
2	little or no variation; some frequent problems in sentence structure	use very limited vocabulary or incorrect word choice	some severe errors
1	demonstrates severe problems in sentence structure	displays numerous errors in vocabulary	contains pervasive errors

How to score your essays: Evaluate your essay in each of the area on the chart. Enter the numbers on the lines below. Then calculate the average of the six numbers to get your score. On the SAT, at least two graders will mark your essay on a scale of 1 to 6, with 6 being the highest. So you may ask a friend or teacher to rate your essay to get your final score.

Self-evaluation (Each area is rated 6 to 1)

Overall impression   _____

Organization and development   _____

Thesis and examples   _____

Sentence structure   _____

Word choice   _____

Grammar   _____

Total   _____

Divide by 6 for your score   _____

Evaluation from a friend or teacher (Each area is rated 6 to 1)

Overall impression   _____

Organization and development   _____

Thesis and examples   _____

Sentence structure   _____

Word choice   _____

Grammar   _____

Total   _____

Divide by 6 for your score

   ▶ cross out the redundancies.

   ▶ smooth out any irrelevant words.

   ▶ check your grammar.

Self-evaluation Chart

	Overall impression	Organization and development	Thesis and examples
6	develops effectively and insightfully a point of view on the issue and demonstrates strong critical thinking; outstanding writing competence; using appropriate examples, reasons to support its position	well organized and thoroughly developed; clearly focused and coherent	demonstrates excellent perception and clarity; original; includes apt and specific facts, examples or references
5	develops effectively a point of view on the issue and demonstrates strong critical thinking; good writing competence; use appropriate examples, reasons to support its position; less incisive and insightful than the highest-scoring essay	well organized and focused; demonstrates coherence and progression of ideas	demonstrates good perception and clarity; includes specific facts, examples or references
4	demonstrates adequate critical thinking; competent writing; includes references and examples	generally organized and focused, demonstrating some coherence and progression of ideas	perceptive and clear; includes facts, examples or references

	Overall impression	Organization and development	Thesis and examples
3	develops a point of view on the issue; exhibits some critical thinking, but may do so inconsistently or use inadequate examples	limited in its organization or focus, or may demonstrate some lapses in coherence or progression of ideas	somewhat clear but with incomplete or confusing thinking
2	develops a point of view on the issue that is vague or seriously limited; demonstrates weak critical thinking; provides inappropriate examples to support its position	poorly organized and/or focused, or demonstrates serious problems with coherence or development of ideas; fail to respond to the issue	very little clarity; irrelevant examples
1	develops no viable point of view on the issue; provides little or no evidence to support its position	disorganized or unfocused	very irrelevant statement or off the topic

	Sentence structure	Word choice	Grammar
6	demonstrates meaningful variety in sentence structure	exhibits skillful use of language, using a varied, accurate and apt vocabulary	virtually error free
5	demonstrates variety in sentence structure	exhibits facility in the use of language, using appropriate vocabulary; a few errors	occasional minor errors
4	demonstrates some variety in sentence structure	exhibits adequate but inconsistent facility in the use of language, using generally appropriate vocabulary	some minor errors

	Sentence structure	Word choice	Grammar
3	lacks variety or demonstrates problems in sentence structure	displays developing facility in the use of language, but sometimes uses weak vocabulary	some major errors
2	little or no variation; some frequent problems in sentence structure	use very limited vocabulary or incorrect word choice	some severe errors
1	demonstrates severe problems in sentence structure	displays numerous errors in vocabulary	contains pervasive errors

How to score your essays: Evaluate your essay in each of the area on the chart.

Enter the numbers on the lines below. Then calculate the average of the six numbers to get your score. On the SAT, at least two graders will mark your essay on a scale of 1 to 6, with 6 being the highest. So you may ask a friend or teacher to rate your essay to get your final score.

Self-evaluation (Each area is rated 6 to 1)

Overall impression   _____

Organization and development   _____

Thesis and examples   _____

Sentence structure   _____

Word choice   _____

Grammar   _____

Total   _____

Divide by 6 for your score   _____

Evaluation from a friend or teacher (Each area is rated 6 to 1)

Overall impression   _____

Organization and development   _____

Thesis and examples   _____

Sentence structure	_____
Word choice	_____
Grammar	_____
Total	_____
Divide by 6 for your score	_____

Practice Essay 4

Directions: Consider carefully the following statement and the assignment below it. Then plan and write an essay that explains your ideas as persuasively as possible. Keep in mind that the support you provide-both reasons and examples-will help make your view convincing to the reader.

> It's not what happens to you that determines how far you will go in life; it is how you handle what happens to you.
>
> - Zig Ziglar

Assignment: What is your view of the idea that attitude determines success and failure? Plan and write an essay in which you develop your point of view on this issue. Support your position with reasoning and examples taken from your reading, studies, experience, or observations.

Follow the steps while writing your essay.

Step 1: Read the prompt carefully and decide your position. (3 minutes)

Decide whether you agree or disagree. you must respond to the assigned topic; you must choose yes or no.

_____

_____

_____

Step 2: Brainstorm your ideas and write the examples you might use in

the space below. (2 minutes)

Vary the examples: pick examples from different category.

_____

_____

_____

Step 3: Write introductory paragraph.(2 minutes)

Do not wander around the topic: clearly introduces the SAT question and your position. Try to catch the interest of the readers.

_____

_____

_____

Step 4: Begin the body.(15 minutes)

Be sure to include at least two examples and it is usually composed of three paragraphs.

Body paragraph 1

_____

Body paragraph 2

_____

Body paragraph 3

_____

Step 5: Write the conclusion.(1 minute)

Repetition can be annoying. Gracefully exit your essay by making a quick wrap-up sentence, and then end on some memorable thought, perhaps a quotation, or an interesting twist of logic, or some call to action.

Step 6: Check and polish.(1 minute)

Gracefully exit your essay by making a quick wrap-up sentence, and then end on some memorable thought, perhaps a quotation, or an interesting twist of logic, or some call to action.

▶ cross out the redundancies.

▶ smooth out any irrelevant words.

▶ check your grammar.

Self-evaluation Chart

	Overall impression	Organization and development	Thesis and examples
6	develops effectively and insightfully a point of view on the issue and demonstrates strong critical thinking; outstanding writing competence; using appropriate examples, reasons to support its position	well organized and thoroughly developed; clearly focused and coherent	demonstrates excellent perception and clarity; original; includes apt and specific facts, examples or references
5	develops effectively a point of view on the issue and demonstrates strong critical thinking; good writing competence; use appropriate examples, reasons to support its position; less incisive and insightful than the highest-scoring essay	well organized and focused; demonstrates coherence and progression of ideas	demonstrates good perception and clarity; includes specific facts, examples or references

	Overall impression	Organization and development	Thesis and examples
4	demonstrates adequate critical thinking; competent writing; includes references and examples	generally organized and focused, demonstrating some coherence and progression of ideas	perceptive and clear; includes facts, examples or references
3	develops a point of view on the issue; exhibits some critical thinking, but may do so inconsistently or use inadequate examples	limited in its organization or focus, or may demonstrate some lapses in coherence or progression of ideas	somewhat clear but with incomplete or confusing thinking
2	develops a point of view on the issue that is vague or seriously limited; demonstrates weak critical thinking; provides inappropriate examples to support its position	poorly organized and/or focused, or demonstrates serious problems with coherence or development of ideas; fail to respond to the issue	very little clarity; irrelevant examples
1	develops no viable point of view on the issue; provides little or no evidence to support its position	disorganized or unfocused	very irrelevant statement or off the topic

	Sentence structure	Word choice	Grammar
6	demonstrates meaningful variety in sentence structure	exhibits skillful use of language, using a varied, accurate and apt vocabulary	virtually error free
5	demonstrates variety in sentence structure	exhibits facility in the use of language, using appropriate vocabulary; a few errors	occasional minor errors

	Sentence structure	Word choice	Grammar
4	demonstrates some variety in sentence structure	exhibits adequate but inconsistent facility in the use of language, using generally appropriate vocabulary	some minor errors
3	lacks variety or demonstrates problems in sentence structure	displays developing facility in the use of language, but sometimes uses weak vocabulary	some major errors
2	little or no variation; some frequent problems in sentence structure	use very limited vocabulary or incorrect word choice	some severe errors
1	demonstrates severe problems in sentence structure	displays numerous errors in vocabulary	contains pervasive errors

How to score your essays: Evaluate your essay in each of the area on the chart. Enter the numbers on the lines below. Then calculate the average of the six numbers to get your score. On the SAT, at least two graders will mark your essay on a scale of 1 to 6, with 6 being the highest. So you may ask a friend or teacher to rate your essay to get your final score.

Self-evaluation (Each area is rated 6 to 1)

Overall impression   _____

Organization and development   _____

Thesis and examples   _____

Sentence structure   _____

Word choice   _____

Grammar   _____

Total   _____

Divide by 6 for your score   _____

Evaluation from a friend or teacher (Each area is rated 6 to 1)

Overall impression   _____

Organization and development   _____

Thesis and examples   _____

Sentence structure   _____

Word choice   _____

Grammar   _____

Total   _____

Divide by 6 for your score   _____

Practice Essay 5

Directions: Consider carefully the following statement and the assignment below it. Then plan and write an essay that explains your ideas as persuasively as possible. Keep in mind that the support you provide-both reasons and examples-will help make your view convincing to the reader.

When written in Chinese the word "crisis" is composed of two characters-one represents danger and the other represents opportunity.

- John F. Kennedy

Assignment: Do people truly benefit from hardships? Plan and write an essay in which you develop your point of view on this issue. Support your position with reasoning and examples taken from your reading, studies, experience, or observations.

Follow the steps while writing your essay.

Step 1: Read the prompt carefully and decide your position.(3 minutes)

Decide whether you agree or disagree. you must respond to the assigned topic; you must choose yes or no.

_____

_____

Step 2: Brainstorm your ideas and write the examples you might use in the space below. (2 minutes)

Vary the examples: pick examples from different category

_____

_____

_____

3: Write introductory paragraph. (2 minutes)

Do not wander around the topic: clearly introduces the SAT question and your position. Try to catch the interest of the readers.

_____

_____

_____

Step 4: Begin the body. (15 minutes)

Be sure to include at least two examples and it is usually composed of tree paragraphs.

Body paragraph 1

_____

_____

_____

Body paragraph 2

_____

_____

_____

Step 5: Write the conclusion. (1 minute)

Repetition can be annoying. Gracefully exit your essay by making a quick wrap-up sentence, and then end on some memorable thought, perhaps a quotation, or an interesting twist of logic, or some call to action.

_____

_____

_____

Step 6: Check and polish.(1 minute)

Gracefully exit your essay by making a quick wrap-up sentence, and then end on some memorable thought, perhaps a quotation, or an interesting twist of logic, or some call to action.

_____

_____

_____

► cross out the redundancies.

► smooth out any irrelevant words.

► check your grammar.

Self-evaluation Chart

	Overall impression	**Organization and development**	**Thesis and examples**
6	develops effectively and insightfully a point of view on the issue and demonstrates strong critical thinking; outstanding writing competence; using appropriate examples, reasons to support its position	well organized and thoroughly developed; clearly focused and coherent	demonstrates excellent perception and clarity; original; includes apt and specific facts, examples or references
5	develops effectively a point of view on the issue and demonstrates strong critical thinking; good writing competence; use appropriate examples, reasons to support its position; less incisive and insightful than the highest-scoring essay	well organized and focused; demonstrates coherence and progression of ideas	demonstrates good perception and clarity; includes specific facts, examples or references
4	demonstrates adequate critical thinking; competent writing; includes references and examples	generally organized and focused, demonstrating some coherence and progression of ideas	perceptive and clear; includes facts, examples or references
3	develops a point of view on the issue; exhibits some critical thinking, but may do so inconsistently or use inadequate examples	limited in its organization or focus, or may demonstrate some lapses in coherence or progression of ideas	somewhat clear but with incomplete or confusing thinking

	Overall impression	**Organization and development**	**Thesis and examples**
2	develops a point of view on the issue that is vague or seriously limited; demonstrates weak critical thinking; provides inappropriate examples to support its position	poorly organized and/or focused, or demonstrates serious problems with coherence or development of ideas; fail to respond to the issue	very little clarity; irrelevant examples
1	develops no viable point of view on the issue; provides little or no evidence to support its position	disorganized or unfocused	very irrelevant statement or off the topic

	Sentence structure	**Word choice**	**Grammar**
6	demonstrates meaningful variety in sentence structure	exhibits skillful use of language, using a varied, accurate and apt vocabulary	virtually error free
5	demonstrates variety in sentence structure	exhibits facility in the use of language, using appropriate vocabulary; a few errors	occasional minor errors
4	demonstrates some variety in sentence structure	exhibits adequate but inconsistent facility in the use of language, using generally appropriate vocabulary	some minor errors
3	lacks variety or demonstrates problems in sentence structure	displays developing facility in the use of language, but sometimes uses weak vocabulary	some major errors
2	little or no variation; some frequent problems in sentence structure	use very limited vocabulary or incorrect word choice	some severe errors

	Sentence structure	Word choice	Grammar
1	demonstrates severe problems in sentence structure	displays numerous errors in vocabulary	contains pervasive errors

How to score your essays: Evaluate your essay in each of the area on the chart. Enter the numbers on the lines below. Then calculate the average of the six numbers to get your score. On the SAT, at least two graders will mark your essay on a scale of 1 to 6, with 6 being the highest. So you may ask a friend or teacher to rate your essay to get your final score.

Self-evaluation (Each area is rated 6 to 1)

Overall impression   _____

Organization and development   _____

Thesis and examples   _____

Sentence structure   _____

Word choice   _____

Grammar   _____

Total   _____

Divide by 6 for your score

Evaluation from a friend or teacher (Each area is rated 6 to 1)

Overall impression   _____

Organization and development   _____

Thesis and examples   _____

Sentence structure   _____

Word choice   _____

Grammar   _____

Total   _____

Divide by 6 for your score   _____

Practice Essay 6

Directions: Consider carefully the following statement and the assignment below it. Then plan and write an essay that explains your ideas as persuasively as possible. Keep in mind that the support you provide-both reasons and examples-will help make your view convincing to the reader.

> Individual commitment to a group effort-that is what makes a team work, a company work, a society work, a civilization work.
>
> - Vince Lombardi

Assignment: Do you think compromise is necessary for successful teamwork? Plan and write an essay in which you develop your point of view on this issue. Support your position with reasoning and examples taken from your reading, studies, experience, or observations.

Follow the steps while writing your essay.

Step 1: Read the prompt carefully and decide your position. (3 minutes)

Decide whether you agree or disagree. you must respond to the assigned topic; you must choose yes or no.

_____

_____

_____

Step 2: Brainstorm your ideas and write the examples you might use in the space below. (2 minutes)

Vary the examples: pick examples from different category

_____

_____

_____

Step 3: Write introductory paragraph. (2 minutes)

Do not wander around the topic: clearly introduces the SAT question and your position. Try to catch the interest of the readers.

_____

_____

_____

Step 4: Begin the body.(15 minutes)

Be sure to include at least two examples and it is usually composed of three paragraphs.

Body paragraph 1

_____

_____

Body paragraph 2

_____

_____

Body paragraph 3

_____

_____

Step 5: Write the conclusion.(1 minute)

Repetition can be annoying. Gracefully exit your essay by making a quick wrap-up sentence, and then end on some memorable thought, perhaps a quotation, or an interesting twist of logic, or some call to action.

_____

_____

_____

Step 6: Check and polish.(1 minute)

Gracefully exit your essay by making a quick wrap-up sentence, and then end on some memorable thought, perhaps a quotation, or an interesting twist of logic, or some call to action.

▶ cross out the redundancies.

▶ smooth out any irrelevant words.

▶ check your grammar.

Self-evaluation Chart

	Overall impression	Organization and development	Thesis and examples
6	develops effectively and insightfully a point of view on the issue and demonstrates strong critical thinking; outstanding writing competence; using appropriate examples, reasons to support its position	well organized and thoroughly developed; clearly focused and coherent	demonstrates excellent perception and clarity; original; includes apt and specific facts, examples or references
5	develops effectively a point of view on the issue and demonstrates strong critical thinking; good writing competence; use appropriate examples, reasons to support its position; less incisive and insightful than the highest-scoring essay	well organized and focused; demonstrates coherence and progression of ideas	demonstrates good perception and clarity; includes specific facts, examples or references
4	demonstrates adequate critical thinking; competent writing; includes references and examples	generally organized and focused, demonstrating some coherence and progression of ideas	perceptive and clear; includes facts, examples or references
3	develops a point of view on the issue; exhibits some critical thinking, but may do so inconsistently or use inadequate examples	limited in its organization or focus, or may demonstrate some lapses in coherence or progression of ideas	somewhat clear but with incomplete or confusing thinking

	Overall impression	**Organization and development**	**Thesis and examples**
2	develops a point of view on the issue that is vague or seriously limited; demonstrates weak critical thinking; provides inappropriate examples to support its position	poorly organized and/or focused, or demonstrates serious problems with coherence or development of ideas; fail to respond to the issue	very little clarity; irrelevant examples
1	develops no viable point of view on the issue; provides little or no evidence to support its position	disorganized or unfocused	very irrelevant statement or off the topic

	Sentence structure	**Word choice**	**Grammar**
6	demonstrates meaningful variety in sentence structure	exhibits skillful use of language, using a varied, accurate and apt vocabulary	virtually error free
5	demonstrates variety in sentence structure	exhibits facility in the use of language, using appropriate vocabulary; a few errors	occasional minor errors
4	demonstrates some variety in sentence structure	exhibits adequate but inconsistent facility in the use of language, using generally appropriate vocabulary	some minor errors
3	lacks variety or demonstrates problems in sentence structure	displays developing facility in the use of language, but sometimes uses weak vocabulary	some major errors

	Sentence structure	Word choice	Grammar
2	little or no variation; some frequent problems in sentence structure	use very limited vocabulary or incorrect word choice	some severe errors
1	demonstrates severe problems in sentence structure	displays numerous errors in vocabulary	contains pervasive errors

How to score your essays: Evaluate your essay in each of the area on the chart. Enter the numbers on the lines below. Then calculate the average of the six numbers to get your score. On the SAT, at least two graders will mark your essay on a scale of 1 to 6, with 6 being the highest. So you may ask a friend or teacher to rate your essay to get your final s core.

Self-evaluation (Each area is rated 6 to 1)

Overall impression   _____

Organization and development   _____

Thesis and examples   _____

Sentence structure   _____

Word choice   _____

Grammar   _____

Total

Divide by 6 for your score   _____

Evaluation from a friend or teacher (Each area is rated 6 to 1)

Overall impression   _____

Organization and development   _____

Thesis and examples   _____

Sentence structure   _____

Word choice   _____

Grammar   _____

Total   _____

Divide by 6 for your score _____

Practice Essay 7

Directions: Consider carefully the following statement and the assignment below it. Then plan and write an essay that explains your ideas as persuasively as possible. Keep in mind that the support you provide-both reasons and examples-will help make your view convincing to the reader.

Practice makes perfect.

- author unknown

Assignment: What's your view of the idea that practice makes perfect? Plan and write an essay in which you develop your point of view on this issue. Support your position with reasoning and examples taken from your reading, studies, experience, or observations.

Follow the steps while writing your essay.

Step 1: Read the prompt carefully and decide your position. (3 minutes)

Decide whether you agree or disagree. you must respond to the assigned topic; you must choose yes or no.

_____

_____

_____

Step 2: Brainstorm your ideas and write the examples you might use in the space below. (2 minutes)

Vary the examples: pick examples from different category

_____

_____

_____

Step 3: Write introductory paragraph. (2 minutes)

Do not wander around the topic: clearly introduces the SAT question and your position. Try to catch the interest of the readers.

Step 4: Begin the body. (15 minutes)

Be sure to include at least two examples and it is usually composed of three paragraphs.

Body paragraph 1

Body paragraph 2

Body paragraph 3

Step 5: Write the conclusion. (1 minute)

Repetition can be annoying. Gracefully exit your essay by making a quick wrap-up sentence, and then end on some memorable thought, perhaps a quotation, or an interesting twist of logic, or some call to action.

Step 6: Check and polish. (1 minute)

Gracefully exit your essay by making a quick wrap-up sentence, and then end on some memorable thought, perhaps a quotation, or an interesting twist of logic, or some call to action.

_____

_____

_____

▶ cross out the redundancies.

▶ smooth out any irrelevant words.

▶ check your grammar.

Self-evaluation Chart

	Overall impression	Organization and development	Thesis and examples
6	develops effectively and insightfully a point of view on the issue and demonstrates strong critical thinking; outstanding writing competence; using appropriate examples, reasons to support its position	well organized and thoroughly developed; clearly focused and coherent	demonstrates excellent perception and clarity; original; includes apt and specific facts, examples or references
5	develops effectively a point of view on the issue and demonstrates strong critical thinking; good writing competence; use appropriate examples, reasons to support its position; less incisive and insightful than the highest-scoring essay	well organized and focused; demonstrates coherence and progression of ideas	demonstrates good perception and clarity; includes specific facts, examples or references
4	demonstrates adequate critical thinking; competent writing; includes references and examples	generally organized and focused, demonstrating some coherence and progression of ideas	perceptive and clear; includes facts, examples or references
3	develops a point of view on the issue; exhibits some critical thinking, but may do so inconsistently or use inadequate examples	limited in its organization or focus, or may demonstrate some lapses in coherence or progression of ideas	somewhat clear but with incomplete or confusing thinking

	Overall impression	Organization and development	Thesis and examples
2	develops a point of view on the issue that is vague or seriously limited; demonstrates weak critical thinking; provides inappropriate examples to support its position	poorly organized and/or focused, or demonstrates serious problems with coherence or development of ideas; fail to respond to the issue	very little clarity; irrelevant examples
1	develops no viable point of view on the issue; provides little or no evidence to support its position	disorganized or unfocused	very irrelevant statement or off the topic

	Sentence structure	Word choice	Grammar
6	demonstrates meaningful variety in sentence structure	exhibits skillful use of language, using a varied, accurate and apt vocabulary	virtually error free
5	demonstrates variety in sentence structure	exhibits facility in the use of language, using appropriate vocabulary; a few errors	occasional minor errors
4	demonstrates some variety in sentence structure	exhibits adequate but inconsistent facility in the use of language, using generally appropriate vocabulary	some minor errors
3	lacks variety or demonstrates problems in sentence structure	displays developing facility in the use of language, but sometimes uses weak vocabulary	some major errors

	Sentence structure	Word choice	Grammar
2	little or no variation; some frequent problems in sentence structure	use very limited vocabulary or incorrect word choice	some severe errors
1	demonstrates severe problems in sentence structure	displays numerous errors in vocabulary	contains pervasive errors

How to score your essays: Evaluate your essay in each of the area on the chart. Enter the numbers on the lines below. Then calculate the average of the six numbers to get your score. On the SAT, at least two graders will mark your essay on a scale of 1 to 6, with 6 being the highest. So you may ask a friend or teacher to rate your essay to get your final score.

Self-evaluation (Each area is rated 6 to 1)

Overall impression   _____

Organization and development   _____

Thesis and examples   _____

Sentence structure   _____

Word choice   _____

Grammar   _____

Total

Divide by 6 for your score   _____

Evaluation from a friend or teacher (Each area is rated 6 to 1)

Overall impression   _____

Organization and development   _____

Thesis and examples   _____

Sentence structure   _____

Word choice   _____

Grammar   _____

Total

Divide by 6 for your score _____

Chapter V

9 SAT essay Topics and Essay Sample Explanation

SAT 作文題目涉及廣泛，包括社會問題、科技發展、資訊媒體、教育與知識、成功與挫折、自我價值等。本章不僅對題目範疇進行分類，以使學生有的放矢地準備素材，而且根據不同範疇的題目類型，給出高分作文或者低分作文，並對作文進行詳解分析，同時針對多篇文章提出寫作注意事項，如：「例證一定與立場緊密相關，才不會離題」，「文章架構是否清晰連貫」。

Section I: Modern Society Issues

Topic 1: Is apathy a problem in today's society?

Think carefully about the issue presented in the following excerpt and the assignment below:

> An entertainment-driven society culture runs the risk of encouraging passivity among its citizens. If they can experience something vicariously through a movie, television show, or video game, why should they get involved with the activity itself? It's safer, after all, to watch someone scale a mountain than to do it yourself. The effect of this passivity, of course, is an

apathetic frame of mind. We cease to care deeply about so many things because they are experienced, at best, second-hand.

Assignment: Is apathy a problem in today's society? Plan and write an essay in which you develop your point of view on this issue. Support your position with reasoning and examples taken from your reading, studies, experience, or observations.

Essay 1

There is no denying the fact that apathy is a problem in today's society. Helen Keller, a true testament to the spirit of activism, supports this axiom by saying, "Science may have found a cure for most evils, but it has found no remedy for the worst of them all- the apathy of human beings." Upon historical consideration, we find it is only in the past few decades that apathy has become an apparent problem. In the past, when freedom of speech and expression was evolving into a cornerstone of society, activism was substantial and every citizen wanted his or her voice to be heard. However, this is not the case today. In modern society, apathy has become chronic, amplified by the increasingly entertainment-driven society that we live in today. This apathy can be attributed to the constant advancement of technology in entertainment, which has caused people to become ignorant and intellectually lazy.

In Canada and the United States, "voter apathy" is the clearest demonstration of a society that is becoming increasingly passive and indolent. Thomas E. Patterson, a Harvard professor of government and the press, recently published The Vanishing Voter, in which "voter apathy" is discussed. According to Patterson, from the years following the Civil War, through the Progressive Era, to the Liberal Era, voter turnout was significantly higher than it is today. The numbers speak for themselves. 65% of the adult population came out to vote in the 1960 presidential election versus 51% in the 2000 election. People had a lot to vote on back in the day: black enfranchisement, labour rights and protection, systems of currency, women's suffrage, to name a few. Every citizen was sincerely concerned, but more significantly, they were informed and ardent. With only the ear and the newspaper as resources for obtaining information, it is ironic how much more aware people were of their country's primary problems and economic situation than our current generation is today.

There is a coherent connection between this ignorance and our growing obsession with technology and entertainment. In the past, when farmers weren't working the fields or when labourers weren't working in the factories, they were socializing in salons, bars, and clubs, and the talk was more than often about a problem with a governmental policy or plans to petition against an unjust amendment. But today, youth are more concerned about when the next episode of Family Guy airs or when the latest generation of the iPod Nano comes out. And when they are not immersed in their solitary world of technological entertainment, their social conversations with friends are next to meaningless, usually about buying something new and unnecessary. Young adults today are so preoccupied with their materialistic and pop-cultural way of life that they have become complacent and delusional; believing that everything is "okay" and the older people will make the right decisions to take care of them. It is this indolent and passive mentality that has contributed to the apathy of our generation's youth.

And even in the face of the portentous global issue of climate change-never mind a country's economic position-young adults in modern society remain passive and ignorant. The belief that most students are greener is a commonly held fallacy. As is evident everywhere across North America, youth at school continue to throw recyclable cans into the trash and many environmental clubs consist of few if no members. Few youth even know what they're own carbon footprint is, a vital step in beginning to take action against global warming. And who can blame them. Why worry about the problems of the adult world when they are blissfully ignorant in a security bubble of constant entertainment and media? Unfortunately, the youth of today will be the leaders of tomorrow and many question whether they can inherit such an overwhelming task.

So consider the older generation's depiction of the youth today. It is most likely an answer of a self-absorbed generation, unperturbed and uninformed of the goings-on around them. As harsh as that sounds, it shows the truth of reality as it is. With so much media influence on entertainment and materialism, young adults have fallen into a subconscious state of popular culture frenzy, becoming passive and apathetic towards momentous issues like climate change and important decisions like voting. If the youth of America were not so oblivious to this entertainment-driven society's subjugation on their free thought, perhaps they would regain that initiative that they no longer share with their parents and grandparents. If those in history least prone to apathy have taught us anything, it is that "you must be the change that you wish to see in the world."

Essay Score: 6

Scoring Explanation

The essay effectively and insightfully develops its point of view that "In modern society, apathy has become chronic, amplified by the increasingly entertainment-driven society that we live in today" through appropriate and reasonable examples. Examples about apathy most writers think of would be students' apathy toward study and their teachers, or teachers' disinterest, lack of dedication, and apathy toward students, or apathy and indifference people have about other people. But the writer of this essay first gives an example of "voter's apathy" with concrete statistics followed by reasonable explanation and argument in the third paragraph by beginning with a topic sentence "There is a coherent connection between this ignorance and our growing obsession with technology and entertainment", which could turn on and impress the readers immediately. Built around the topic sentence in the third paragraph, the writer makes good argument to support the point by saying "youth are more concerned about when the next episode of Family Guy airs or when the latest generation of the iPod Nano comes out. And when they are not immersed in their solitary world of technological entertainment, their social conversations with friends are next to meaningless···Young adults today are so preoccupied with their materialistic and pop-cultural way of life that they have become complacent and delusional; believing that everything is "okay" ··· It is this indolent and passive mentality that has contributed to the apathy of our generation's youth." The essay ends with a summary of the reasons and restatement of the position.

So the essay exhibits a command of thinking and writing skills.

1. proficient, coherent development of a position on the topic

2. relevant evidence to support its position

3. well-ordered progression from idea to idea

4. varied sentence structure and free from technical flaws

One minor mistake is the essay is a bit long. Yes. Research has found that 90% of essays over 400 words in length receive the highest score of 12. But it cannot be too long. This essay is around 700 words and some statements could be omitted such as the one in the beginning paragraph: "Upon historical consideration, we find it is only in the past few decades that apathy has become an apparent problem. In the past, when freedom of speech and expression was evolving into a cornerstone of society, activism was substantial and every citizen wanted his or her voice to be heard. However, this is not the case today."

Suggestion to readers:

Critical thinking! Organization! Well-founded examples and evidence!

Essay 2

A young boy of approximately six or seven is crouched in front of the computer screen, intent on the prey before him. A man of twenty or so is pacing nervously along the dimly lit corridor, the details of his face visible despite the lighting. The detail of his clothing and weapon are also incredible, giving him a three-dimensional, realistic look. He had an almost human air of worry and distress etched on his face as he paced along, when suddenly BANG! The man's shocked features burst into a splash of blood and gore. The now headless man slowly sinks to the ground, a broken island in as sea of his own spreading blood. And what of the boy watching the death? "Yes!" He shouts triumphantly, punching his fists in the air as the message "Head Shot" appears on the screen.

Indeed, in our entertainment-driven society today, apathy is a widespread phenomenon, because it distances people from reality. Examples of this include online conversations, the usage of social networking sites, and the well-known Bystander Effect.

Online conversations on messengers like MSN or YAHOO promote apathy by distancing face-to-face interaction between people. You cannot truly tell if a particularly caustic comment made by your friend is a joke or not, and the trite letters "jk" which denote just kidding are equally as lacking in meaning, these sorts of conversation are encouraging feelings of indifference about other people, which, as a study conducted in 2007 about teens talking online found, promotes apathetic thoughts in a person. Because there is no emotional connection to words spoken online, teens also learn to disregard emotion in social interactions.

The phenomenon is also found on social networking sites like Facebook and Twitter, which objectify people's lives. People update their statuses, or tweet about their lives, which other people can then reply to. Once again, the lack of any emotional or real connection to these events encourages teens to disregard them in real life. For example, a person who tweets on Twitter about getting cut is likely to get just as many sardonic, mean comments as sympathetic comments, which goes to show apathetic nature of the Internet.

Finally, perhaps the best example of the apathy that is permeating society is the Bystander Effect. This effect decides the apathy of bystanders when they see a crises unfolding or a victim getting publicly abused. This phenomenon came to the public eye when a girl named Kitty Genorese was raped and stabbed to death by a series killer even though numerous people saw her condition and heard her pleas of help. Nobody came to save her, however, as each bystander thought somebody else would come forth to save her. Even more recently, a young African American was beaten to death by a gang in front of a large apathetic crowd. In each case, the indifference and passivity of the crowd resulted in the murder of the victim.

Apathy is becoming a growing problem in today's society, encouraged by the growing divide between true social interactions and online conversation and networking as well as video gaming. Such indifference is threatening to tear apart our society as people become withdrawn from the realities of our society. The Bystander Effect and the death of Kitty Genorese are haunting examples of the effects apathy has in modern society.

Essay Score: 6

Scoring Explanation

The writer creatively begins writing the introduction by describing a scene of a boy playing gun shot game, which would probably pluck up the spirits of the readers. The writer then clearly demonstrates the point that "In our entertainment-driven society today, apathy is a widespread phenomenon, because it distances people from reality." The writer exhibits outstanding critical thinking by giving three well-founded examples: online conversations, the usage of social networking sites, and the well-known Bystander Effect. The essay is well organized and clearly focused, displaying clear coherence and smooth progress of ideas. The essay also exhibits skillful use of language, using a varied, accurate and apt vocabulary and demonstrates meaningful variety in sentence structure.

Essay 3

Sitting banally in a chair and watching someone doing things on TV. People start to connect with the outside world less virtually and more electronically.

Technology is taking over the society and making it apathetic as shown through literature and real life.

In The Veldt, two children is raised by a computer-simulated character so they are apathetic to their real and biological parents. Their nursery can create 3D images from their thoughts. Thus, instead of actually going out and experience the nature, they painstakingly construed a real African jungle through their imagination. With this advanced technology, the kids became apathetic towards the nature as well as their parents' feelings. When the parents decide to shut down the nursery because it is taking over too much of the children's life, the children lock them in the nursery simulated jungle where the lion devoured their parents. (The kids made a few alternations) Technology made these kids detached and apathetic to the real world, to others' life and feelings.

Apathy also results from daily use of technology in real life. Don't you feel offended when people bump into you without saying sorry because they are text-messaging? Don't you wish that drivers would not talk on their phones when they are on the road? Don't you want teenagers to take out their earplugs when they are talking to you? New technological gadgets draw people more into their own world. They become more introverted, self-centered and apathetic towards others. They disregard others' feelings and build fragile relationship via Internet. After all, why would one waste the time on the road to talk face-to-face with a friend when one can talk online? When friends are in need, they need the virtual, warm presence of anther friend to support them. Certainly not a few dismissive and consolating phrases. People who connect electronically only show apathy.

Technology is advancing at an alarming rate. It quickly permeates into every aspect of society-talking, online messaging, and listening to music··· Technology is making apathy a growing problem in today's society and we need to set aside the new gadgets sometimes and experience the magic of the real world around us.

Essay Score: 4

Scoring Explanation

The writer doesn't read the prompt carefully. As in the assignment, it says: "An entertainment-driven society culture runs the risk of encouraging passivity among its citizens. If they can experience something vicariously through a movie, television show, or video game···" So if the writer focused on the point of "entertainment-driven society" rather than "technology" , the essay would have received a score of 5. But still, the essay shows skill in responding to the question, "Is apathy a problem in today's society?" In the beginning of the essay, and the rest of the discussion does convey reasons to support the position. The ideas are also logically grouped with conclusion offered. The essay shows variety in sentence structure and generally free of most errors in grammar and usage.

Suggestion to readers:

Focus on the issue

Topic 2: Is the world changing for the better?

Think carefully about the issue presented in the following excerpt and the assignment below:

"There is, of course, no legitimate branch of science that enables us to predict the future accurately. Yet the degree of change in the world is so overwhelming and so promising that the future, I believe, is far brighter than anyone has contemplated since the end of the Second World War."

-Adapted from Allan E. Goodman, A Brief History of the Future: The United States in a Changing World Order

Assignment : Is the world changing for the better? Plan and write an essay in which you develop your point of view on this issue. Support your position with reasoning and examples taken from your reading, studies, experience, or observations.

Essay 1

The many changes that the world is currently undergoing will have a mostly positive effect on the future. Though there are a few negative trends (terrorism, global warming, etc.), I am confident that the world is still moving forward. I believe that the world is changing for the better because of three observations.

Our technology is always improving. It is often said that 90% of the most revolutionary technological breakthroughs have occurred in the past 100 years. Judging by the speed at which our personal gadgets (cell phones, computers, GPS systems) become atavistic junk, the rate of improvement will not slow down anytime soon. Technology is not only becoming more advanced, it is also becoming more affordable. Even in poverty stricken countries, nearly everyone has a cell phone nearby for emergencies. Obviously, this illustrates the immediate positive impact of our improving technology.

Governments around the world are also improving. Huge changes in the ways countries are run occur every day. When India became a capitalist economy in the late 1900s, the positive impact circumnavigated the globe. As more and more people yearn for democracy, the closer the world will get to being one ruled by the many, not the few. As government types and market systems have their inadequacies ironed out, the magnanimous effect will be ubiquitous.

Finally, the world is becoming a better place because people of all types are starting to come together. The world is becoming a global community, largely due to the increase in technology and changes in governing systems, and as this occurs, differences will be set aside. Hopefully, as the many members of the many nations around the world come together, peace will ensue.

As evidenced by improving technology, changing governments, and global togetherness, the world is changing for the better. Our grandchildren will have better lives than did anyone before them.

Essay Score: 4

Scoring Explanation

The essay supports its position that "The many changes that the world is currently undergoing will have a mostly positive effect on the future" through three examples: technology, changing governments, and global togetherness, which exhibits a generally dependable command of writing and thinking skills, despite some mistakes along the way. When giving the benefits of technology, it would be better if it could give a list of what the benefits would be and how they change the world for the better, rather than simply focusing on cell phones, which makes the argument weak. Sentence structure and word choice are consistently simple, with sentences repeatedly beginning with, "I think," "I know," "I believe," or "I am confident."

Suggestion to readers:

Use reasonable examples and don't use such phrases as "I think," "I know," "I believe," or " I am confident."

Essay 2

As the world's technological advances save more lives and raise the quality of living globally, the world is still rapidly declining in other areas. Today environmental problems, political conflict, and the decay of society plight the world. Since World War II pollution levels have skyrocketed and the environment has been disregarded, a move which has led to global warming and the extinction of many species. Political conflicts have led to strained international relations and the innocent deaths of thousands of civilians while the problems seldomly are resolved. Society, primarily the youth, face more problems than ever. Depression and drug use are on the rise while body image and family values are declining. all three of these factors change the world, but definitely not for the better.

Environmental issues did not begins, but were fueled by the roaring industrial revolution in the early 1900s. Pollution from new factories filled the air and streams in cities while farmers multiplied the size of their farms in the countryside vie the acquisition of virgin tracts of land. Expansion confined animals to small areas that could not support them, causing the extinction of some species. Many of these problems have been identified and resolved in the United States, however in third world and underdeveloped countries these environmental issues are still prevalent. The most prevalent of these problems is the shrinking of the South American rainforest, a major contributor to global warming. The possible effects of global warming include melting of the ice caps, which would cause catastrophic flooding. These environmental struggles do not benefit the world.

Political conflict is another source of negative developments in the world. Conflicts over land and power have resulted in strained international relations, most notably in the Middle East and Africa. the central governments of these areas are not strong enough to squash the rebellions and end the violence. Foreign intervention just stirs up both sides of the issue rather than resolve them because many politicians have motives other than peace. Today, politicians appeal to the passions of the populations that vote for them, and do not focus on real issues. It is therefore impossible for the public to be overly surprised with what politicians do internationally because they never asked about his policy in the first place. Political corruption has led to a decay in society.

The youth of society in particular have been affected by modern day problems. Girls feel pressure to look like airbrushed images on billboards while boys are encouraged to disrespect women in songs and on TV. Drug use and depression have both skyrocketed in recent years in response to social pressures. The media's overwhelming influence distorts the youth's idea of what society is really like. The next generation will be further influences by the current youth and the pattern may either break or repeat. As of right now, all levels of society are being negatively impacted.

Unless the environment, politics, and society are directly targeting in an effort to make changes for the better, society will continue in the deteriorating pattern it is in currently. If world changes continue in this manner, the world will continue to change for the worse and not for the better.

Essay Score: 5

Scoring Explanation

The argument demonstrates clear and consistent mastery. The writer effectively develops the point of view that "As the world's technological advances save more lives and raise the quality of living globally, the world is still rapidly declining in other areas." By focusing on environmental issues, political conflicts and society, the writer supports the thesis and demonstrates critical thinking. But the political conflict example is not elaborated well. "Conflicts over land and power have resulted in strained international relations, most notably in the Middle East and Africa. The central governments of these areas are not strong enough to squash the rebellions and end the violence. Foreign intervention just stirs up both sides of the issue rather than resolve them because many politicians have motives other than peace." A more concrete example is required here, and therefore, helps strengthen the thesis more. Language usage errors are frequently distracting such as "seldom" (misspelled as "seldomly"). Some words are not used appropriately and accurately like "plight," and "prevalent;" some words are unnecessary, for example, in stead of saying "the youth of society," use "youth."

Suggestion to readers:

When use big words, use them appropriately and accurately.

Essay 3

The world is changing for the better. The world has changed drastically over the last few decades and has led us to a brighter future. This can be seen in technology, politics, and personal betterment.

Technology has come a long way in the last ten years alone, the advancements are astounding. Almost every month there is a new iPod, a faster computer, and a fancier cell phone. The world has gone wireless and it has never been easier to stay connected. Electronic books are now beginning to emerge just adding to the list of great achievements in technology. All of this contributes to the betterment of the world, keeping people connected and updated on what is going on around them.

After six years of occupying land in the Middle East, the United States government is finally making plans to withdraw troops from Iraq. No one can say that their time there was wasted but the time has come to let the Iraqi people live their lives without US occupation. The Taliban controlled the people in a harsh dictatorship and now there is a raw form of democracy.

Personal betterment is yet another way in which the world is changing for the better. For example, Francie Nolan in A Tree Grows in Brooklyn is a young girl destined to grow up and live in poverty all her life. However, Francie takes it upon herself to visit the public library often and read books nondiscriminately. Through the advancement of her mind, Francie does well in school and even gets and job later in life.

The world is constantly changing. Whether it be advancements in technology, politics, or self, these changes occur everyday. No one can predict the future, but when contemplated we can see it is bright ahead.

Essay Score: 3

Scoring Explanation

The essay is organized and focused. It develops a point of view in the very beginning that "The world is changing for the better" and demonstrates competent thinking. The weakness of the essay is about the examples. First, the writer gives a list of technology advancements: "···every month there is a new iPod, a faster computer, and a fancier cell phone. The world has gone wireless and it has never been easier to stay connected. Electronic books are now beginning to emerge just adding to the list of great achievements in technology." The writer then adds that "All of this contributes to the betterment of the world." The statement about new technology advancements are only facts and they are meaningless, since the readers expect to be convinced how these advancements and staying connected are bettering the world. So the reader needs to know that you can list facts and examples, but don't forget to elaborate them and comment. Second, the info presented on the Iraqi war is weak, too. Whether US politics getting to Iraqi affairs is good or not still remains discussed. Does it make the world better? Perhaps there is no answer yet. Third, Francie Nolan does not fit the topic since she is getting better doesn't necessarily mean that the world is changing for better unless you explain people like her today can improve themselves with grants allowing people to go to college.

Suggestion to readers:

Use appropriate examples.

Topic 3: Should modern society be criticized for being materialistic?

Think carefully about the issue presented in the following excerpt and the assignment below:

> Materialism: it's the thing that everybody loves to hate. Few aspects of modern life have been more criticized than materialism. But let's face it: materialism-acquiring possessions and spending money-is a vital source of meaning and happiness in our time. People may criticize modern society for being too materialistic, but the fact remains that most of us spend most of our energy producing and consuming more and more stuff. Adapt-

ed from James Twitchell, Two Cheers for Materialism.

Assignment：Should modern society be criticized for being materialistic? Plan and write an essay in which you develop your point of view on this issue. Support your position with reasoning and examples taken from your reading, studies, experience, or observations.

Essay 1

Modern society shouldn't be criticized for being too materialistic. Pocessions tell a story about how successful a person has been in life. The more pocessions one has, the more successful and happier they appear. However, this should not be the case. I have met people throughout my life who prove that our society should be criticized for being materialistic. My uncle Bob lives in a small house, without much modern technology; but he lives a great life.

My uncle lives with his wife in a small cottage near Lake George, New York. He lives a peaceful life without much need for many materials. He does not own a television or a computer. He is happy to live off the land without being obsessed over buying new things. He does not have to be materialistic, because he can live off the land with just a few supplies. Unlike many in our society, my uncle does not go out and buy new items right when they hit the market. Even if he needs something, he will wait until the price drops and most likely something better has come out before he gets it. My uncle lives a great and carefree life without many processions. My family is another example of having a happy life without materials.

For generations, my family has farmed the land to produce our wealth. We have lived in this same location for over one-hundred years. Occasionally, we will purchase a new tractor or combine to help with the work, but this is very rare. The tractor we currently use is fifteen years old. My father and I have repaired it ever since I was a little kid. Our life is great because we do not live in a heavily populated area, and we are free from the materialism of or society. When we travel, I am amazed at all the unnecessary materials that people own. It seems that they just want to try and "keep up with the Jones" . I do not understand why every one needs these materials when my life is so great without them. I agree with James Twitchell when he said "··· most of us spend most our energy producing, and consuming more and more stuff." However, I hope that in the next couple decades, our society will realize what necessities really are.

If our society became less materialistic, it would help every part of our lives. People like my uncle live healthy lives free from stress. My family is able to have a carefree attitude about life, and enjoy the little things that make us smile. If more people were like this, our society would not be violent as it is today. I hope that someday, our society will fall away from materialism, and not take for granted the processions they already have.

Essay Score: 4

Scoring Explanation

The response of the essay to the issue is "I have met people throughout my life who prove that our society should be criticized for being materialistic." However, the examples are not strong enough to prove the thesis. The writer gives two examples, both about his family, to illustrate that people who have carefree attitude about life and don't take possessions granted are happy. And the writer is "amazed at all the unnecessary materials that people own." On one hand, to some degree, yes, the writer supports the thesis by telling the readers that his or her uncle and family are happy although they don't have much possession. On the other hand, however, does it mean that people who have much possession and live successful lives are not happy? Does it mean people who are being materialistic are not happy? Or does it necessarily mean that people who are rich are not happy because of being materialistic or something else? So the examples are not well-grounded and seem to be weak. There are some sparkling statements in the essay such as "why every one needs these materials when my life is so great without them" and "our society will realize what necessities really are" . The essay doesn't exhibit facility in the use of language and doesn't demonstrate variety in sentence structure.

Suggestion to readers:

Make your statements meaningful.

Essay 2

Society's devolution from nomadic to modern has left a gap that remains open. Modern society has attempted to repent for its shift by creating a never ending prosperity: materialism. The infinite cycle of buying has create a never closing gap in society to allow for the forbidden vices to prosper under false pretenses. If our quest for getting meaningless resources continues, what will we have left inside?

Exulted by the late 50s, capitalism has given rise to an epidemic-the "individual". The emphasis on the individual has justified countless acts of greed, ambition and envy. Materialism feeds into the selfish souls who are praised and held up by modern society. How can we find happiness if we only look at our impulse wants and our own selfish desires?

The never ending quest to acquire the best and the most has create the rise of the Machiavellian individual-willing to do anything to get what they want. As shown by the popular teen series, Gossip Girl, girls will do anything to achieve ends' meet. Blaire's own ambition to get into Yale entices her to seduce her own interviewer and cheat in school. Her own desire to be admitted into a prestigious college pushes over the ethical limits of academics and mortality. But even the desire to have the 'right' clothes has influenced many to steal from stores.

Materialism has brought out the exact vices our ancestors strove to ban. Even the Ten Commandments tell us not to lust after what we can't have. But the increasingly cynical market attempts to make us lust after every product/service advertised-so we buy it.

This never ending bombardment of advertisements has often attacked by myriad of parents and rational advocates of children. The real question remaining now is: Will children in this generation retain good morals if materialism overpowers the exact beliefs entwined in us by religion?

As drugstores increase their assortment of beauty products, the choices increase. But, how perfect can be if makeup can't hide our innermost vices? Materialism has taken us too far from the beginnings of it in the 1900s. As shown by Fitzgerald's The Damned and the Beautiful, perfectionism is impossible. If we depend on products to fulfill our desires, what is left? In our modern age, there's little left as fashionistas are considered to be the role models of countless students in schools.

The tragic shift in modern society has created an empty gap that can be only be filled by perfecting the soul, not the body. Before materialism takes over every aspect of society including religion, its necessary to stop the vices and learn that the soul cannot be clothed or made-up; the soul can only be fulfilled.

Essay Score: 5

Scoring Explanation

This essay shows great understanding of the writing task. The writer takes a position on the issue (Society's devolution from nomadic to modern has left a gap that remains open. Modern society has attempted to repent for its shift by creating a never ending prosperity: materialism) and offers context for discussion by illustrating specific reasons and examples. The essay demonstrates coherence and progression of ideas through its series of acts about people's greed, ambition and envy. The essay also uses language effectively ("As drugstores increase their assortment of beauty products, the choices increase. But, how perfect can be if makeup can't hide our innermost vices?" and "The tragic shift in modern society has created an empty gap that can be only be filled by perfecting the soul, not the body."). To achieve a higher score, the essay needs to focus on one example and elaborate the weaknesses of being too materialistic. Besides, the sentence Gossip

Girl, girls will do anything to achieve ends' meet" has been overstated. One cannot say girls from "Gossip Girl" will do anything to achieve ends' meet. "Anything" is too extreme.

Section II: Technology "Advancement"

Topic 1: Do the benefits of technology always outweigh the costs?

Think carefully about the issue presented in the following excerpt and assignment below.

"You, on the cutting edge of technology, have already made yesterday's impossibilities the commonplace realities of today. Why should we start thinking small now? In protecting mankind, I think we must be ambitious. If science has taught us anything, it's taught us that-well, it's not to be modest in our aspirations. "

- Adapted from Ronald Regan

Technology…is an odd thing. It brings you great gifts with one hand, and it stabs you in the back with the other. It is only by the rational use of technology; to control and guide what technology is doing; that we can keep any hopes of a social life more desirable than our own.

- Adapted from C. P. Snow

Assignment : Do the benefits of technology always outweigh the costs? Plan and write an essay in which you develop your point of view on this issue. Support your position with reasoning and examples taken from your reading, studies, experience, or observations.

Essay 1

As I banged my head on the table in frustration at the computer that would not start up, my accounting teacher said to me, "a computer is as good as the person using it," as she pointed to the unplugged cable of the monitor. From this experience, I disinterred the notion that a tool is useful only if it is used purposefully and not fallaciously.

Many have held technology as the culprit for many of today's problems. Such problems include: invasion of privacy, antisocial behavior in adolescents, greater access to immoral material and a loss of appreciation for mundane pleasure. "Face-time" is also replaced more by emails and instant messenging, and more people are beginning to tune out the world, while tuning into their music.

Although these changes in lifestyle is evident, are these problems really caused by the tool (technology), or the wielders of the tools (people)? Many of these problems surface through the abuse of technology, rather than technology itself. For example, the invasion of privacy is preventable if measures are taken to protect it. Also, antisocial behavior is only caused by secluded usage of technology for long duration of time. If moderation is taken into concern, adolescents can learn to monitor time spent in front of a radiation-emitting screen to balance the time given to physical social contact.

Therefore, technology is not the cause of sin, but rather, a tool, like any other tool, that can bring joy if used effectively and moderately.

Sample Score: 5

Scoring Explanation

This essay effectively develops the point of view that "Technology is a useful tool only if it is used purposefully and not fallaciously." The writer demonstrates critical thinking by clearly focusing on if negative side of technology is "caused by the tool (technology) or the wielders of the tools (people)" . The writer begins by giving a vivid description of a"computer event" , by which she clearly makes her position. The writer then lists today's problems caused by technology include: "invasion of privacy, antisocial behavior in adolescents, greater access to immoral material and a loss of appreciation for mundane pleasures." Then the writer explains "Many of these problems surface through the abuse of technology, rather than technology itself" by demonstrating three examples to support the position. The essay is well organized, demonstrating clear coherence and smooth progression of ideas. Throughout the essay, the writer exhibits the skillful use of language by using a varied, accurate vocabulary although there is one subject-and-verb-agreement mistake (Although these changes in lifestyle is evident). It is supposed to be these changes in lifestyle are evident. The essay would be scored six if the writer added some benefits of technology, making the argument more comprehensive.

Suggestion to readers:

When the essay question lists two sides of one thing, you are asked to make a comparison or judgment. So don't forget to describe both of the sides mentioned in the prompt.

Essay 2

The world that humanity resides in now is a grandiose display of a few millenia's worth of progress. Looking back at the past, we can only begin to imagine the envy of our forebears. Were they able to witness this world of fantasies? Technology is the "odd thing" that propels the foundations of this world forward. Technology has never ceased to appall the awestruck people with its infinite showcase of the gamut from luxuries to necessities. Humans are benefiting at every turn from the onset of new technological advances. Although friction will result at first, technology brings unimaginable prosperity to mankind.

"Necessity is the mother of invention," states Archimedes. The telegram, the telephone, and finally the Internet have astonishingly linked people from around the globe. Ideas are shared, information is released, and relationship between friends and family are strengthened. Without the technology of telecommunication, the world to an individual would be shrouded in darkness, and the marvelous opportunities we now have would be non-existent to that unfortunate individual. Technology has given us a medium for knowledge, and invaluable thing.

Technology is also saving lives. In the form of surgery, people that would have died in the absence of high-tech tools will now survive to see another sunrise. Surly for those who are blessed with a second chance at life, technology is a vital aspect in our lives.

Evidently, technology is a blessing that empowers our lives. The short-duration of unfamiliarity with some technology is greatly overshadowed by this beacon of possibilities. In fact, technology is nothing short of a landmark of our existence.

Sample Score: 4

Scoring Explanation

The question the writer was to address was not "What are some benefits of technology?" but, rather, "Do the benefits of technology always outweigh the costs?" The writer lists a series of benefits from technology; he doesn't explain why the benefits should be greater than the drawbacks. This is a deadly mistake the writer made. In the essay, he only mentions the drawback once. He wrote in the introduction paragraph that "Although friction will result at first, technology brings unimaginable prosperity to mankind." However, he doesn't elaborate what the friction would be and of course there will be no judging in detail whether the benefits outweigh the drawbacks. But we have to say the same sentence saves him from going too far from the topic as he made his position in a different way that benefits of technology do outweigh the costs. The writer also exhibits his good command of language skills by using varied sentence types and appropriate vocabulary. He made one spelling mistake in the word, "millennia" , which he missed an "n" , but one mistake like this can be negligible.

Suggestion to readers:

Always remember to make a clear position in the first paragraph. Or, in other words, answer the question.

Essay 3

"Technology is an odd thing." I think the benefits of technology don't always outweigh the costs. With the advancement in technology, people become lazier and lazier. The ycan even shop and get whatever they want without leaving their homes. For example, online shopping was becoming more and more popular recently. People could buy things and have them delivered to their homes with a single click on the mouse. More and more people now stayed home without going out for days. Social interactions were omitted if everybody just stayed at home. It is the "social interactions" that distinguish humans from robots. A movie has been made in the last few years, expressing concerns for excessive use of technology. The movie showed a group of humans on a giant space ship. These humans lose the ability to walk and move their body because the crew members who are all robots do everything for them.

The other problem created by technology is pollutions. Cars produce large amount of air pollutions. In addition to cars, factories are also a large threat to the environment. Factories not only create air pollution problems, sometimes they contaminate water sources as well. One most dangerous thing technology has created is nuclear-generated power station. If an accident occur in any of the processes during nuclear fusion, the whole station faced the charge of exploding. Accompanied the explosion would be a release of large amount of radioactivity. The radioactivity could kill people as well as injure them. Babies can be mutated and everything would be contaminated by radioactivity. People would have to abandon their homes.

A final problem is that when a technology falls into the wrong hand, they could become weapons against human race.

Sample Score: 4

Scoring Explanation

This essay is also scored 4 but for a different reason. The writer makes direct and clear position in the beginning of the essay and points out powerful examples to support the point of view. Different from the first and the second essay, the writer describes both the benefits and drawbacks, and explains why the former doesn't always outweigh the latter in detail. However, the weakness is deadly in the essay. There is some organization to the essay, but nothing very clearly done: introductory paragraph includes position followed by examples in detail, ideas are not logically grouped, conclusion is not conclusion since it raises a new question, which the writer doesn't have time to explain.

Suggestion to readers:

Organization, organization and organization.

Topic 2: Do changes that make our lives easier not necessarily make them better?

Think carefully about the issue presented in the following excerpt and assignment below.

Technology promises to make our lives easier, freeing up time for leisure pursuits. But the rapid pace of technological innovation and the split second processing capabilities of computers that can work virtually nonstop have made all of us feel rushed. We have adopted the relentless pace of the very machines that were supposed to simplify our lives, with the result that, whether at work or play, people do not feel like their lives have changed for the better.

- Adapted from Karen Finucan, Life in the Fast Lane

Assignment: Do changes that make our lives easier not necessarily make them better?

Essay 1

Change is inevitable in our lives. As a result, we constantly ask ourselves whether change is for the better or for the worse. In today's society, many changes captivate our attention with the enticing promise of making our lives easier; however, easier does not necessarily mean better. Examples from history and literature show us why.

The Industrial Revolution brought upon Europe a new perspective on technological change. The creation of never before seen machinery, in its initial debut, gave rise to the popular belief that life would be easier, and also much better. In reality, millions of workers, though now employed, worked under horrendous conditions, and the increase of factories contributed to the smog that suffocated many cities. Despite recent technological advances, modern society is not facing a revolution, perse, but there is question as to whether we are or will be facing similar consequences, except incompatibility to modern standards. In its extremities, we can reference a dystopian society depicted in literature.

In Ray Bradbury's "Fahrenheit 451", the main character, Guy Montag lives in a society "advanced" to the point of regression: Classic forms of entertainment, such as books, are banned, replaced by two-line synopses and the fictional characters playing out scenes on a "wall", an animation of sorts, in which the spectator can seem to take part. It sounds familiar, because they are only further advances to the "conveniences" we see today: book reviews or cliff notes, and the well-loved television screen.

"If life is passing by too quickly, slow down." As can be inferred from the quote, change is constantly happening around, but ultimately, we can make the decision as to how relevant change is, and how we let it influence our lives.

Sample Score: 5

Scoring Explanation

The writer makes clear position in the beginning of the essay that "many changes captivate our attention with the enticing promise of making our lives easier; however, easier does not necessarily mean better." Two examples, one from history and one from literature, the writer then displays, support the position. The essay concludes with a quote "If life is passing by too quickly, slow down," which metaphorically points out that "change is constantly happening around, but ultimately, we can make the decision as to how relevant change is, and how we let it influence our lives." So the essay shows good organization and logical development. The essay also exhibits skillful use of language and demonstrates meaningful variety in sentence structure. The weakness of the essay is about the example. When the writer explains "In reality, millions of workers, though now employed, worked under horrendous conditions," the essay doesn't clarify this point, making the argument weak.

Suggestion to readers:

Clarify your examples.

Essay 2

Although technology promises to make our lives easier, it doesn't necessarily make them better. Technology causes people to work in a rush. A computer can process a giant calculation in a split second and work nonstop. When a person is using the computer, he/she is likely to adopt the pace of the computer. The result is simple. People feel more tired. I once read a biography of a writer. He claimed, before the invention of computers, I feel less pressure because I can jog down my thoughts and have a flexible writing schedule. But now, whenever I sit in front of my computer staring at the blank screen, I feel that I have to writer something, at least a short passage to fill up the screen. Even when I don't have inspiration, I feel rushed to type something.

In addition to that, technology damages our living environment. When walking on streets, the air isn't fresh anymore. This causes a rise in lung disease in the more heavy-polluted countries. Technology innovations, such as cars, factories and so on worsens people's living environment while making lives easier. Many villages that are close to a contaminated water source has to walk miles just to get fresh water. You can feel that different by simply walking in a street in big cities in China and then a street in country side of China. Before I moved to Canada, my dad would take my family to country sides of China. There life is simple and most importantly the air is fresh.

In addition to rushing people and creating pollution, technology also made people too reliable on it. Now almost every industry uses some sort of technology. I heard about a company having an technical problems. Its whole computer system was hacked, all their data was lost. Luckily, the company was small and it had a back-up system. However, it still took all the employees a whole month before they reorganize all the data when people are reliable on technology and a technical problem occur, it created a lot of inconvenience.

Technology does make people's lives easier in some ways. However, it creates more problems. It creates pollution, rushes people and makes people too reliable.

Sample Score: 4

Scoring Explanation

There is a position on the issue in the beginning of the essay (Although technology promises to make our lives easier, it doesn't necessarily make them better.) , the rest of the discussion partially convey reasons to support that position. Some statements supporting claims are not understandable (A computer can process a giant calculation in a split second and work nonstop. When a person is using the computer, he/she is likely to adopt the pace of the computer. The result is simple. People feel more tired.) Would it seem to be technology's fault when they adopt the pace of the computer and they feel tired? The writer doesn't show variety of examples. Two of them are the experiences from the writer's own or the writer's friend, and the third one is something that the writer has heard about, making the argument not convincing. The writer also makes too many grammatical errors. For example, "Many villages that are close to a contaminated water source has to walk." Can villages walk and since the subject is plural, shall we use have?

Suggestion to readers:

Show variety in your examples.

Topic 3: Have modern advancements truly improved the quality of people's lives?

Think carefully about the issue presented in the following excerpt and the assignment below.

The advancements that have been made over the past hundred years or more are too numerous to count. But has there been progress? Some people would say that the vast number of advancements tells us we have made progress. Others, however, disagree, saying that more is not necessarily better and that real progress-in politics, literature, the arts, science and technology, or any other field-can be achieved only when an advancement truly improves the quality of our lives.

Assignment: Have modern advancements truly improved the quality of people's lives? Plan and write an essay in which you develop your point of view on this issue. Support your position with reasoning and examples taken from your reading, studies, experience, or observations.

Essay 1

Countless of advancements were made during the past hundred years, but whether these advancements truly improved our life qualities is fiercely debated. Internet, for example, on one hand, brings us convenience and mass information, while on the other hand, if abused, can cause great harm to our society. Despite the flaw it has, Internet still benefit us in a great many ways, thus improving the standards of our lives.

When the Internet, or World Wide Web, first introduced into China in 1987，it was only used and tested in China's Academy of Sciences. In 1994, it was more use in educational system. With the progress of informationization, the net is applied to commercial use while still remained unfamiliar to common Chinese people. It was only in 2003 when SARS-a fatal epidemic-hit China did the Internet become popular throughout the country. In order to hide from the airborne disease, millions of people started to communicate online by using instant message tools such as MSN, ICQ and so on; merchants began to make business by using e-shops like EBay and Joyo; students began to take classes by studying online through many online courses. Today, almost everyone in China can get access to the Internet easily and among which many rely on it to study, to work and have fun.

Internet is a powerful tool that combines both convenience and informativeness by which we could know the world without even leaving our houses. If I'm hungry, I can order a meal online; if I'm lost in a strange land, I could simply check out the map on Google; if I miss my sister who is far in America, I can reach her through Email or MSN.

The advancement of such technology indeed improved our lives. However, some people might say that the Internet crime does harm to our society, other complain that the net brings porn stuff to our kids and some think online games can make people addict to it. While the development of technology might have contributed to some of these contemporary problems, it offers the most likely solutions to many of them. In conclusion, modern advancements like the Internet truly improved the quality of people's lives.

Essay Score: 3

Scoring Explanation

The writer doesn't answer the question directly and clearly. The writer demonstrates in the introductory paragraph that "whether these advancements truly improved our life qualities is fiercely debated." But the essay topic is a "Yes" or "No" question. The writer is supposed to tell the readers if he or she agrees or not. Although the examples given present the writer's position, but examples are here for supporting the position not for showing a position. The example shown in the second paragraph doesn't support the position well, either. Describing the development and popularity of Internet in China doesn't necessarily mean it would make people's lives better. For example, "almost everyone in China can get access to the Internet easily and among which many rely on it to study, to work and have fun." Do people relying on Internet to study, to work and have fun mean Internet has improved the quality of people's lives? Graders would not be convinced by the example and statement like this. As for language, the essay contains an accumulation of errors in grammar, usage and mechanics.

Suggestion to readers:

Use adequate examples, reasons to support its position.

Section III: Media and information

Topic 1: Do violence and immorality in the media make our society more dangerous and immoral?

Consider carefully the issue discussed in the following passage, then write an essay that answers the question posed in the assignment:

> Many among us like to blame violence and immorality in the media for a "decline in morals" in society. Yet these people seem to have lost touch with logic. Any objective examination shows that our society is far less violent or exploitative than virtually any society in the past. Early humans murdered and enslaved each other with astonishing regularity, without the help of gansta rap or Jerry Bruckheimer films.

Assignment: Do violence and immorality in the media make our society more dangerous and immoral? Write an essay in which you answer this question and discuss your point of view on this issue. Support your position logically with examples from literature, the arts, history, politics, science and technology, current events or your experience or observation.

Essay

The man in the polished-looking navy blue suit and impeccable tie stepped carefully through the mud along the banks of the river. His glamorous face wrinkled in disgust as he and a police officer looked at the scene of the crime. "Definitely a homicide." He says in calm, assured voice as if that statement justified everything. Half an hour later, the cool-headed investigator turned out to be correct, once again.

CSI, like many other products of the media aims to produce an "authentic" view of criminal investigations and scenes of violence, reflecting the mood of the country and the interest of the audience. To declare that a show like CSI would make modern society more dangerous and immoral is ridiculous. The media's certainly not the one at fault here, as it merely conveys the wishes of the public. Rather, it was in the societies and civilizations of the past without the media that violence and immorality was far more prevalent.

Looking at the very beginning of civilization, it becomes clear that violence was so prevalent that it became almost a necessity as one of the few ways to survive. Nomadic tribes hunting animals would clash over who received the greatest share of the kills, and when agriculture was introduced some ten millennia ago, the violence was shifted to the control of land for farming.

The Sumerians, the members of the first Kcuvukuazation came and went as they were captured by Babylonia in the 2nd and 3rd millennia BC. Next came the Persians, who conquered the crumbling Babylonian Empire. And finally came the Muslims, who, in aquick but bloody war, took over all of Persia in the seventh century AD. Numerous smaller conflicts took place in these eras, all concentrated in what is now referred to as the Cradle of Civilization. Mesapotamia (Mesopotamia). This was merely one region in the world out of many. The Greeks and the Romans occupied the Meditteranean, while the wild Gothic and Celtic peoples ruled Northern Europe before coalescing into individual empires. History itself is a series of conquests and rebellions, bloodshed and warfare. The programs, in the media today are nothing compared to what happened in history. Modern society may well be "drowning in its sorrows" with help from the media,but it is certainly not becoming more dangerous and immoral.

Essay Score: 5

Scoring Explanation

With very interesting and eye-catching opening, this essay generally develops the main idea. (The media's certainly not the one at fault here, as it merely conveys the wishes of the public. Rather, it was in the societies and civilizations of the past without the media that violence and immorality was far more prevalent.) It also consistently displays skillful use of language and meaningful variety in sentence structure. Some spelling mistakes like Mesapotamia, (Correct: Mesopotamia) and Meditteranean (Mediterranean)can be negligible.

However, one weakness about the essay is describing the bloodshed and warfare in the ancient times doesn't prove that the media today doesn't make our society more dangerous and immoral. In other words, you can say A is wrong, but it doesn't prove that B must be wrong.

Suggestion to readers:

Focus on the point.

Topic 2: Do newspapers, magazines, TV, radios determine what is important to most people?

Think carefully about the issue presented in the following excerpt and the assignment below:

> "The media not only transmit information and culture, they also decide what information is important. In that way, they help to shape culture and values."

> - Adapted from Alison Bernstein

Assignment: Do newspapers, magazines, television, radio, movies, the Internet, and other media determine what is important to most people?

Essay

In modern society, people gain most of their information through the media, such as the newspaper, the radio and the television. Some people believe that the media shapes the values of most of us because people tend to pay more attention to the information that the media focuses on. As far as I am concerned, the media doesn't decide what is important to the majority. Indeed, the media tell us what they think can attract our attention, but it does not mean that the information is really important to us.

For example, the media always puts much emphasis on the personal life of Paris Hilton. People are overwhelmed by the news headlines on her every day. But does it mean that her information is of significant to the society or worths our attention. No. Who cares who she dates with! Who cares she was sent to jail for her violation of driving! Who cares she publicized her sexual tape! Most of the news has nothing to do with us and is of no value to the society. Though the media pay much attention to her, her personal life is worthless to the majority. In other words, what the media regards as newsworthy is not necessarily important to most people.

On the other hand, what the media always ignores is sometimes of valuable to people. Phum, a small town in the southern area of Cambodia, is a place where people are so poor that they are even unable to afford the food. In the last few years, we strove to obtain information of this small town. To our disappointment, the media never pay any attention to those people who struggle to survive. Although the media put little emphasis on them, their information is of great value to the people who want to know more about them and to help them.

The examples above demonstrate that it is we rather than the media that decide what is important to us.

Essay Score: 4

Scoring Explanation

This essay demonstrates skill in responding to the task. The writer takes a position (the media doesn't decide what is important to the majority.) and offers some context for the discussion. Development of ideas is adequately done, with ideas discussed with some specific examples and details (the media always puts much emphasis on the personal life of Paris Hilton. People are overwhelmed by the news headlines on her every day. But does it mean that her information is of significant to the society or worths our attention). But sentence structure and word choice are consistently simple. Language usage errors are frequently distracting and contribute to difficulty in understanding some portions of the essay such as "It is of significant (correct: It is of significance)," and "who cares who she dates with (correct: who cares who she dates)."

Suggestion to readers:

Improve your language ability and practice.

Section IV: Individuality and group

Topic 1: Is it always best to determine one's own views of right and wrong, or can we benefit from following the crowd?

Think carefully about the issue presented in the following excerpt and the assignment below.

> We do not take the time to determine right from wrong. Reflecting on the difference between right and wrong is hard work. It is so much easier to follow the crowd, going along with what is popular rather than risking the disapproval of others by voicing an objection of any kind.

> - Adapted from Stephen J. Carter, Integrity

Assignment: Is it always best to determine one's own views of right and wrong, or can we benefit from following the crowd? Plan and write an essay in which you develop your point of view on this issue. Support your position with reasoning and examples taken from your reading, studies, experience, or observations.

Essay 1

In our world today, everyone is offered choices, often between two extremes: hot or cold, black or white, and so forth. Similarly, there is a constant battle between our presumed right and wrong. People think there is a definition to "right" and "wrong" , the "real" meaning, and while some are willing to find that denotation, others would just rather follow the crowd.

First of all, is there really right and wrong? Or are they abstract concepts formed in our minds to justify actions and words? Sigmund Freud believed, for example, that one part of our mind, the id, represented our most primitive selves, barbarians who would go to any cost to apply basic survival skills, while the ego forced us into reality, and the superego acted as the judge. Though Freud's theories

146

have some truth, countless other psychologists have come to conclusion that his theories were not accurate. This forces us to the conclusion that right and wrong is within our ability to change.

Many of the social changes in history happened because people believed that the crowd was wrong, and moreover, did something about it. William Still, Harriet Tubman, and other abolitionists believed black slavery was wrong, and risked their lives to help thousands of blacks to freedom. Later on, Martin Luther King Jr. continued to dream of a world of coexistence; he, too, had contributed greatly towards it. Gandhi changed the minds of others in a peaceful way. Nellie McClung fought for women's rights in Canada. All these people believed that what society considered right was wrong; they chose to go against the crowd.

"If your friends jumped off a cliff, would you do it, too?" It is very likely easier to go with the crowd, but our society isn't what it is today because it was convenient.

Essay Score: 4

Scoring Explanation

With interesting argument and examples, the essay displays unique critical thinking. Instead of directly responding to the issue by deciding if it is always best to determine one's own views of right and wrong or we can benefit from following the crowd, the opening of the essay describes people's different understanding of what "right" and "wrong" are.

However, the explanation that "right" and "wrong" are, perhaps, abstract concepts, as Freud believed "the id, represented our most primitive selves, barbarians who would go to any cost to apply basic survival skills, while the ego forced us into reality, and the superego acted as the judge" in some way, confuses readers as it jumps quickly to another conclusion that "right and wrong is within our ability to change."

The third paragraph begins with statement "Many of the social changes in history happened because people believed that the crowd was wrong, and moreover, did something about it," with a list of examples, and ends in "All these people believed that what society considered right was wrong; they chose to go against the crowd," which develops the idea "This forces us to the conclusion that right and wrong is within our ability to change," given in the second paragraph.

Unfortunately, the essay comes to conclusion without an ending, perhaps because of the limited time, leaving the argument weak.

Throughout, the essay exhibits skillful use of language and demonstrates meaningful variety in sentence structure. (Sigmund Freud believed, for example, that one part of our mind, the id, represented our most primitive selves, barbarians who would go to any cost to apply basic survival skills, while the ego forced us into reality, and the superego acted as the judge.)

Suggestion to readers:

Build a direct and clear relationship between the statement and the thesis. And remember that an unfinished essay is not penalized for lacking a full conclusion, but if it is not developed, it will be.

Essay 2

North America is a society filled with uniqueness. One has his or her own lifestyle, taste and even personal system of judgement. One who develops his or her own determination of a situation is sometimes lauded at for his or her uniqueness. However, one's determination of right or wrong is often influenced by a general judgement of the public, and one benefit from following the crowd.

Take a new born baby, for example. Fresh into the world, how is he or she able to tell good from bad, conscientious from immoral, and beauty from ugliness? Psychological studies have shown that a child's judgement of beauty correlates with that of the parent. In everyday, through our observations, we can also see that a violent child also has a violent parent, and that both the parent and the child think that violence is something morally acceptable. At a young age, one develops one's own judgement, influenced by the parent and by a larger crowd. Such influence is usually beneficial to the child. A parent often tries to present the best qualities to the child. The child, using what he or she learns from the parent as a basis may develop his or her own criteria for determining good and bad.

As a grown person, it is also beneficial to follow the crowd's opinion. As the crowd slowly accept Galileo's theory of the sun being the centre of the solar system, one who has one's own judgement of the matter may choose to adhere to his own opinion or follow the idea of the crowd. The latter choice, recognized by the public, is often right. By following this choice, one benefits since he or she gains a new piece of knowledge that was not available to him or her.

Following the crowd is not as bad as it seems in the multifarious North America. It is instead beneficial. However, one has to make sure the one follows the "right" crowd.

Essay Score: 4

Scoring Explanation

This essay demonstrates adequate mastery in developing its point of view. (one's determination of right or wrong is often influenced by a general judgement of the public, and one benefit from following the crowd.) The essay displays competent critical thinking in providing several adequate examples of people who are beneficial because of following the crowd, from new born babies to the grownups. The essay is adequately organized and displays some progression of ideas. The essay also exhibits adequate facility in the use of language. To achieve a higher score, the essay needs to illustrate statements more appropriately and effectively (In everyday, through our observations, we can also see that a violent child also has a violent parent, and that both the parent and the child think that violence is something morally acceptable. The statement is not appropriately given and too extreme), make fewer mechanical errors (it is "judgment" , not "judgement" . All spellings of the word "judgment" are wrong in the essay), anddon't use "he or she" or "him or her" too many times in one essay.

Suggestion to readers:

Watch your spelling and grammar.

Topic 2: Is there any value for people to belong only to a group or groups with which they have something in common?

Think carefully about the issue presented in the following excerpt and the assignment below.

Since we live in a global society, surely we should view ourselves as citizens of the whole world. But instead, people choose to identify and associate with smaller and more familiar groups. People think of themselves as belonging to families, nations, cultures, and generations-or as belonging to smaller groups whose members share ideas, views, or common experiences. All of these kinds of groups may offer people a feeling of security but also prevent them from learning or experiencing anything new.

Assignment: Is there any value for people to belong only to a group or groups with which they have something in common? Plan and write an essay in which you develop your point of view on this issue. Support your position with reasoning and examples taken from your reading, studies, experience, or observations.

Essay 1

Although being diverse can be beneficial to one's own knowledge and experience, one is more often able to achieve values and employ his strengths in a group with which he has something in common. Canadian youth rights activist Craig Kielburger and Indian Independence leader Mohandas Gandhi are exemplary of how people can be valuable in a homogeneous group.

At the age of twelve, Craig Kielburger was touched by a newspaper article he read in which an Indian boy of his age was shot for speaking up for child rights. After extensive research and teaming up with friends who, like him, feel strongly about the cause, Kielburger established Free The Children. Together with his friends, he persevered to spread their shared belief and instigate action around the world, by exposing the horrors of rights, and demonstrating how they can stop child labor, Craig and his team gained prominent support worldwide. Free The Children works to this day to promote the cause of child rights. Thus, through believing in the same cause and working hard to achieve their goal, Craig Kielburger and his group of friends successfully went into action and ameliorated the lives of millions of children.

Similarly, Indian independence and rights activist Mohandas Gandhi obtained his goal of freeing India from control of Britain through cooperating with his followers and fellow believers. One of Gandhi's most audacious movements was the salt protest, where he demonstrated civil disobedience by picking up a handful of salt from the British-controlled Indian beach. Eventually, by acting with civil disobedience and believing in non-violence as a means of achieving peace, and ultimately independence, Gandhi and his fellow believers gained international support and thus, were finally able to obtain their goal by working together and showing the same values.

Essay Score: 4

Scoring Explanation

The essay uses examples from Craig Kielburger's Free The Children and Gandhi's independence action to support the idea that "Although being diverse can be beneficial to one's own knowledge and experience, one is more often able to achieve values and employ his strengths in a group with which he has something in common." However, the first example isn't used appropriately. Craig's gaining prominent support worldwide after extensive research and teaming up with friends seems to be a good example for proving a thesis about success and adversity, who strives to achieve a goal no matter how hard it is, rather than an example for proving that one is more often able to achieve values for belong only to a group or groups with which they have something in common. The essay demonstrates coherence and progression of ideas. The essay also uses language effectively.

Suggestion to readers:

Focus on the point and use reasoning and well-founded examples.

Topic 3: Are organizations or groups most successful when their members pursue individual wishes and goals?

Think carefully about the issue presented in the following excerpt and the assignment below.

Organizations or groups that share a common goal often mention teamwork as their secret to success by insisting that people in the group work together for the good of the entire group. However, by requiring each individual to accept the decisions of the others in the group, organizations may discourage the expression of individual talent.

Ultimately, a group is most successful when all of its members are encouraged to pursue their own goals and interests.

Assignment: Are organizations or groups most successful when their members pursue individual wishes and goals? Plan and write an essay in which you develop your point of view on this issue. Support your position with reasoning and examples taken from your reading, studies, experience, or observations.

Essay 1:

The uniquely human capacity for group organization and collective action indeed is responsible for much of humanity's triumphs. However, groups do not function at an optimal level when their individual parts work for a good other than that of the group. Rather, all people work towards one unified goal in the ideal group. The ultimate failure of the French Revolution and the origins of the Cold War support this assertion.

The French Revolution, a tempestuous social evolution that shook the foundations of Europe's class structure, saw the unification of the peasants and the upper middle class against the aristocracy that, for centuries, had maintained a foothold on society. Although the Revolution achieved an ephemeral sort of success, it ultimately became a bloody blunder as it devolved into the now infamous Reign of Terror, only to have another tyrant ascend to the throne in its wake. Why? Because the peasants and the upper middle class had different, irreconcilable goals. The peasants sought to ameliorate the poverty and destitution that plagued their lives at the base of the social pyramid. The upper middle class-doctors, lawyers, and bankers-intended to inherit the same status that the aristocrats once held. Over time these disparate goals caused much dispute, gave rise to much dissent, and left the country in a state of intellectual destitution and moral bankruptcy for both classes.

Less than two centuries later, yet more political disaster resulted from the inclusion of two inherently incompatible goals into one group. During World War II, the democratic United States and the communist Soviet Union joined under one political banner in order to effectively combat the Fascist hydras brewing in Germany and Italy. However,as the war drew to a close and each side's military encircled Hitler's Berlin, it became clear as day that two incompatible goals had managed to slip into the Allied Alliance: both the Soviets and the Americans wanted control of Germany after the War. Mutually aware of this, both sides rushed into Berlin to fill the avoid after the Nazi surrender, resulting in the polarized West and East Germany's and ultimately in the Cold War. Had both nations been truly working toward one goal, Fascism would have still been dismantled but the decades of nuclear Fear and mutually-assured destruction might have never been.

Groups, despite the intuitive belief to the contrary, are most effective not when their members pursue individual goals but when their members work toward a common goal. Both the French Revolution and the rise of the Iron Curtain evince this.

Essay Score: 6

Scoring Explanation

Demonstrating outstanding critical thinking, this essay effectively and insightfully develops the point of view that "groups do not function at an optimal level when their individual parts work for a good other than that of the group." Using the clearly appropriate extended examples of "the ultimate failure of the French Revolution and the origins of the Cold War," the essay is well organized and clearly focused as it illustrates the ultimate moral bankruptcy for the peasants and the upper middle classes because of their dispute for disparate goals although they used to team up against the aristocracy, and the relationship between the United States and the Soviet Union. The response displays clear coherence and smooth progression of ideas. The essay also exhibits skillful use of language, using a varied, accurate, and apt vocabulary, and meaningful variety in sentence structure is evident (Although the Revolution achieved an ephemeral sort of success, it ultimately became a bloody blunder as it devolved into the now infamous Reign of Terror, only to have another tyrant ascend to the throne in its wake.). Demonstrating clear and consistent mastery, this essay merits a score of 6.

Suggestion to readers:

Cultivate reading habit and think when you read.

Section V: Honesty

Topic 1: Are people bound to tell the truth at all times, or are there situations in which it is better to lie or tell only partial truths?

Think carefully about the quote and the assignment below.

Honesty is the cornerstone of all success, without which confidence and ability to perform shall cease to exist.

- Mary Kay Ash, founder of Mary Kay Cosmetics, Inc.

Assignment: Are people bound to tell the truth at all times, or are there situations in which it is better to lie or tell only partial truths? Plan and write an essay in which you develop your point of view on this issue. Support your position with reasoning and examples taken from your reading, studies, experience, or observations.

Essay 1

"I'm sorry to inform you Arisa that your father passed away last day." This phrase may likely be a crushing blow to the person receiving it. Often in life, we are faced with situations in which we feel would be better to offer comfort through concealing the truth. Yet, have we considered if hiding the truth behind a mask really would help a person? Lies can only cover the truth of situations for not so long, so it is better for people to tell the truth at all times, as doing so would free us from lay building pains and hurt others less.

Hiding the truth sometimes cause us greater pain and regret that may follow us for the rest of our lives. For example, in the Batman movie, the main character, Bruce Wayne, aka Batman is held back from facing the truth of his parents' death by his own nagging fear of guilt; because he thinks that it was his fault they were killed. This inability to brace what he thought to be their reason for his parents' deaths causes him increasing guilt over the issue. Later, when Bruce has finally decided to accept the "truth," he is surprised and relieved to find that he was not the reason of their misfortune. As it is said "and you will know the truth and the truth will set you free!"

Telling the truth may also reduce the amount of pain caused to other people as a result of lies. For example, if the mother of a girl told her that her father died in a car crash when he actually commited suicide- that girl would live in ignorance of the truth of the situation. But this lie may not be able to be contained forever, and sooner or later, when the girl finds out how her father died-will she not be hurt from the lies all the more? So in this case, will partial truths, it is appropriate to find a suitable manner in which to present the truth.

These examples show that anything but the truth will sooner or later has a negative effect on a person. Rather, by confronting them with the truth, it is easier for them to cope with situations.

Essay Score: 5

Scoring Explanation

This essay supports the thesis that "Lies can only cover the truth of situations for not so long, so it is better for people to tell the truth at all times, as doing so would free us from lay building pains and hurt others less." The examples, from the movie, Batman, about Bruce's changes from fearing of facing the truth to deciding to accept the truth, and from a presupposition about a girl's situation, support the idea that hiding the truth sometimes causes us greater pain and regret and "by confronting them with the truth, it is easier for them to cope with situations." Both examples are explained well in the context of the thesis. The essay is well-organized and provides logical transitions within and between paragraphs.

However, the diction and syntax the writer uses demerit the score. To achieve a higher score, the essay needs to use language more effectively, and make fewer mechanical errors. In "Often in life, we are faced with situations in which we feel would be better to offer comfort through concealing the truth" , "would be" is unnecessary as "we" is already the subject, "feel" is the verb, and "in which" works as adverbial. In "Hiding the truth sometimes cause us greater pain and regret that may follow us for the rest of our lives" , there is a disagreement between the subject "hiding the truth" and the verb "cause" . The writer needs to use "causes" . In the same sentence, "that may follow us for the rest of our lives" is meaningless as the rest of the discussion doesn't mention this point at all.

Suggestion to readers:

Make your statements concise and come to the point.

Essay 2

I think people aren't bound to tell the truth at all times. There are always situation in which one should better lie or tell only partial truth. Even though some people think "Honesty is the cornerstone of all success, without which confidence and ability to perform shall cease to exist," sometimes truth can hurt people.

In some situations people tell "white lies" to encourage others. I've read a true story about a little boy and his mother. The boy's mother had a car accident and her legs were cutted off. The litter boy was depressed so he became a "bad" boy. He failed all his tests, he never completed his homework and he bullied his classmates. All his teachers were worried but no matter what they did, the boy wouldn't listen. Then a new teacher was assigned to the boy's class. The class had a test that day, and the boy failed as usual. After class was over, the new teacher asked the boy to go to her office. The boy thought he was getting punished, but instead, the new teacher gave him a box of his favorite chocolate. She told him, "You did a great job today on your test." The boy was surprised, but he ran home happily, yelling to his mom, "Mother, mother. I did well on my test today and I got a box of chocolate from the new teacher." The mother kissed his cheek and congratulated him. Afterward, whenever he finished his homework or did a test/quiz, the teacher gave him chocolate. And surprisingly, the boy started doing his homework, and he did well on all his tests and quizzes. The boy later got accepted into the best private high school in the province. Once he got the acceptance letter, he bought a box of chocolate and ran to inform his teacher. The teacher was happy for him and she told him the truth, "All the chocolate I gave you was bought by your mother, and you didn't even pass on his old tests and quizzes. Your mother told me to lie to you. Sorry." The boy walked home slowly, crying as he pictured his mother driving her own wheelchair everyday, just to get him a box of chocolate to encourage him. After reading the story, I realized that the boy wouldn't have become successful if his mother had never lied to him about his test and quiz scores, and he wouldn't be encouraged if his mother didn't lie to him about the chocolate.

Essay Score: 3

Scoring Explanation

The essay demonstrates some critical thinking in developing a point of view (I think people aren't bound to tell the truth at all times. There are always situation in which one should better lie or tell only partial truth⋯truth can hurt people). Offering one reason about the boy's progress encouraged by the "white lie" , the essay features some organization and coherence. However, the reason is over developed with a long passage of description of the story itself, which is supposed to be concisely and succinctly displayed with appropriate comment. The essay sometimes uses weak vocabulary and lacks variety in sentence structure. To achieve a higher score, the essay needs to use more competent critical thinking and improved language facility to offer stronger support for its position.

Topic 2: Can deception-pretending that something is true when it is not-sometimes have good results?

Think carefully about the issue presented in the following excerpt and the assignment below.

There are two kinds of pretending. There is the bad kind, as when a person falsely promises to be your friend. But there is also a good kind, where the pretense eventually turns into the real thing. For example, when you are not feeling particularly friendly, the best thing you can do, very often, is to act in a friendly manner. In a few minutes, you may really be feeling friendlier.

- Adapted from a book by C. S. Lewis

Assignment: Can deception-pretending that something is true when it is not-sometimes have good results? Plan and write an essay in which you develop your point of view on this issue. Support your position with reasoning and examples taken from your reading, studies, experience, or observations.

Essay 1

Although deception is more often regarded as detrimental and abominable, it can sometimes be justified and have good results. The novel The Last Leaf and the play Hamlet are paragons of how lying can engender a favorable outcome.

In The Last Leaf by O'Henry, the protagonist Johnsy is debilitated by the outbreak of pneumonia in her village. Convinced that she will die soon, she lies in bed everyday despite her friend Suze's incessant attempts to restore hope in her. Johnsy stares at a vine of ivy leaves outside her window, believing that the falling of the last leaf will signify the end of her life. In desperation, Suze tells their neighbor Mr. Behmrman, who is an old painter barely making a living. He dies during the night when Johnsy is about to give up all hope. However, in the next morning, Johnsy sees the last ivy leaf still hanging onto the vine. Now imbued with hope and confidence, she decides to fight for her life and eventually succeeds. In the end, Johnsy and Suze discover that the last ivy leaf is a painting by Mr. Behrman. He worked with such determination and perseverance to make the picture seem real that he died of exhaustion during the night. Evidently, Mr. Behrman saves Johnsy's life through deceiving her, showing that deception can have good results.

Similarly, the play Hamlet by William Shakespeare proves that lying and misleading can be justified. When his uncle Claudius murders his father, Prince Hamlet of Denmark determines to condemn Claudius by pretending to be psychologically mad. As a result, when Hamlet imitates the scene in which his uncle kills his father, Claudius expresses his indignation and thus, reveals his guilt by storming out of the room. As a result Hamlet succeeds through deception in bringing his uncle to justice and achieves a favorable outcome.

Therefore, The Last Leaf by O'Henry and the play "Hamlet" by Shakespeare demonstrate that deception can, in fact, have good results.

Essay Score: 4

Scoring Explanation

This essay demonstrates adequate mastery in developing its point of view (Although deception is more often regarded as detrimental and abominable, it can sometimes be justified and have good results.). The essay displays competent critical thinking in providing two adequate examples of deception sometimes leading to good results, one from a novel and one from a play. The essay is adequately organized and displays some progression of ideas. The essay also exhibits adequate facility in the use of language.

Ending is weak as it is simply a repetition of the previous statements.

Suggestion to readers:

Simple repetitive statements in the concluding paragraph make your essay weak.

Essay 2

Conscience often tells us that we should not deceive others, and that we should tell the truth. Although such sentiment holds true in most cases, we must also recognize that deception can sometimes yield to good results, in special cases.

One example is the case of young Franklin Roosevelt. Roosevelt, unable to walk in a young age, was introvert in his abled siblings' presence. To plant more confidence in his son, Roosevelt's father called a tree-planting contest among Roosevelt's siblings. In the end, Roosevelt won the contest because his tree grew to be the tallest. Amazed by this surprising outcome, Roosevelt realized that he had the power to accomplish something. Since then, he gained more confidence. However, Roosevelt's winning was a result of his father's deception: his father planted the tree for his son. Such deception had wonderful outcome: Roosevelt came to be the president of the United States.

Roosevelt's father isn't the only one deceived others for a good cause. The famous detective, Sherlock Holmes, depicted in Conan Doyle's book does the same. Whenever Sherlock Holmes encounters the villain of a crime, he uses the powerful tool of deception. After verifying the villain's identity, he pretends to befriend the villain. His pretension led to a good outcome as well: the villain trusts him and eventually fell into his trap.

Recognizing that deception can lead to good outcomes sometimes, we can choose our words carefully in order to lead to a desired effect. However, as our conscience tells us, we have to ensure that effect of deception is a moral one, or else we should not deceive others at all.

Essay Score: 5

Scoring Explanation

This focused essay demonstrates strong critical thinking in developing its point of view (we must also recognize that deception can sometimes yield to good results, in special cases.). The essay uses reasoning and appropriate examples from Franklin Roosevelt and Sherlock Holmes to support the idea that deception can yield good results. The essay demonstrates coherence and progression of ideas. The essay also uses language effectively (Roosevelt's winning was a result of his father's deception: his father planted the tree for his son. Such deception had wonderful outcome: Roosevelt came to be the president of the United States.). To achieve a higher score, the essay needs to elaborate or point out how Holmes powerfully uses deception to lead to good outcomes.

Suggestion to readers:

Make your example concrete and explain.

Topic 3: Do circumstances determine whether or not we should tell the truth?

Think carefully about the issue presented in the following excerpt and the assignment below.

It is often the case that revealing the complete truth may bring trouble -discomfort, embarrassment, sadness, or even harm - to oneself or to another person. In these circumstances, it is better not to express our real thoughts and feelings. Whether or not we should tell the truth, therefore, depends on the circumstances.

Assignment: Do circumstances determine whether or not we should tell the truth? Plan and write an essay in which you develop your point of view on this issue. Support your position with reasoning and examples taken from your reading, studies, experience.

Essay

Telling the truth is obligatory thing to do, especially when this concerns people who are close to you: relatives, friends, family···However, there are certain times when we should keep that truth for ourselves. But we should not lie either. We have to judge on the situation which we are in.

Suppose that you are visiting friend which is suffering from the death of family member. Your friend recently have attempted to pass the exam. You got the results first and your friend have no idea whether he passed it or not. What should you do? The best way is not to mention the exam. But what if he asks about it? You should either delicately change the topic or say that you do not know the results yet.

Imagine another situation: your friend has just had a new haircut. He asks you how he looks. Which option do you think is better: telling the truth or lying? Well, you know your friend better than I do and I cannot tell you what to do, but if I were you, I would surely tell him that he looks fine. It is not really lie, is it? You just keep your opinion to yourself in order not to insult your friend.

These are just examples of situations when we should not tell truth. In real life there are lots of situations when we have to decide whether to tell the truth or not. However, there are certain situations when we should tell the truth no matter how hard it is. I have one particular situation. Your relative has just done his or her blood test and somehow you got the results first. The results are frustrating: he or she has a cancer. Now you have the dilemma: be sincere or wait till the last moment. This is the situation when you MUST tell the truth. No matter how grievous it is, the person who is sick must know that he is sick!

Circumstances definitely determine whether truth should be told or not. There are certain situations when it is better to hide the truth for a while as well as tell it instantly. We should follow our heart to determine which situation is which.

Essay Score: 2

Scoring Explanation

This essay demonstrates inconsistent skill in responding to the task. The writer takes a position (there are certain times when we should keep that truth for ourselves...We have to judge on the situation which we are in.) but displays no recognition of a counter-argument to that position. The essay needs to outline what circumstances dictate telling lies, for example, is it acceptable if one tells lies when no one gets hurt?

The language of the essay is at times confusing and irrelevant to topic. In the opening sentence, for example, "Telling the truth is obligatory thing to do, especially when this concerns people who are close to you: relatives, friends, family···" Does it mean telling the truth is not obligatory thing if it doesn't concern people who are not close to you?

And it seems family is more close to "you" than "relatives," generally speaking. So the word order needs to be changed to "family, relatives, friends···"

There is some organization in structure but nothing very clearly done. The essay displays very little facility in the use of language, using very limited vocabulary. It contains many errors in grammar and mechanics. In the second paragraph, for example, "Suppose that you are visiting friend which (Correct: who) is suffering... Your friend recently have (Correct: has) attempted to pass the exam. You got the results first and your friend have (Correct: has) no idea whether he passed it or not. What should you do (This sentence is meaningless.)? The best way is not to mention the exam. But what if he asks about it (Very weak statement.)? You should either delicately change the topic or say that you do not know the results yet."

Suggestion to readers:

Create a reasonable argument.

Section VI: Education and knowledge

Topic 1: Is education primarily the result of influences other than school?

Think carefully about the issue presented in the following excerpt and the assignment below.

The education people receive does not occur primarily in school. Young people are formed by their experiences with parents, teachers, peers, and even strangers on the street, and by the sports teams they play for, the shopping malls they frequent, the songs they hear, and the shows they watch. Schools, while certainly important, constitute only a relatively small part of education.

Assignment: Is education primarily the result of influences other than school? Plan and write an essay in which you develop your point of view on this issue. Support your position with reasoning and examples taken from your reading, studies, experience, or observations.

Essay

Admittedly, school influences people in many different ways, such as academic knowledge, social activities, and other students' stuff. However, the importance of schooling is outweighed by that of other experiences beyond school, like going to Africa to visit young patient suffering from AIDS, and wandering around the yard in the soft moonlight to gain inspiration of composing songs.

Going to the place where people lead a strenuous life as well as experiencing the pain from diseases does help us realize that we should appreciate the happy life we are leading, and to what extent we are supposed to contribute ourselves to the society. Lady Diana Frances Spencer, Princess of Wales, is remembered more for her beauty, kindness, humanity, and charitable activities than for her technical skills. I admire her for her visit to Africa during which she shook hands with children who got AIDS and also respect her for her ignorance of the royal contentment of her kindness towards the poor. As an aristocrat, she could live economically amply without such care of other arduous people; however, she pursued spiritual intactness which ties her heart to that of all. Since such pursuit of complete soul is rarely taught in school, we learn it from our daily like little by little.

How to live, which we accumulate from our own experiences outside school is no wonder more essential than make a living, which we are taught in school every day. As a part of how to live, besides taking care of others, drawing inspiration from life also plays an indispensible role in our lives. Wandering around the yard and being bathed in the pure moonlight does provide people a unique feeling unlike that in an overcrowded and noisy morning. Ludwig van Beethoven, one of the greatest composers in human history, once heard a conversation between a blind girl and her mother while walking. The blind girl's ardent love of piano, revealing in lines of the conversation and the serene moonlight pouring out from the sky at the horizon aroused Beethoven's inspiration and stimulated him to produce the famous work-Moonlight Sonata. How to seek inspiration through the combination of love and nature can hardly be learned through professors' lectures, but using our hearts to feel and to appreciate.

To sum up, school is crucial in people's life, yet not the most important and influential part of human life. School is a place where we use academic knowledge to better understand the world and sublimate our souls.

Essay Score: 3

Scoring Explanation

This essay demonstrates generally adequate command of writing and thinking skills, although they are typically inconsistent in quality. Taking the position that the importance of schooling is outweighed by that of other experiences beyond school, the essay then gives examples of the experience of Diana's visit to Africa and Beethoven's inspiration of his famous work, Moonlight Sonata. However, the former example doesn't respond to the topic. The topic sentence of the second paragraph is "Going to the place where people lead a strenuous life as well as experiencing the pain from diseases does help us realize that we should appreciate the happy life we are leading." If the writer gave an example showing what he or she has learned though his or her personal experience of "going to the place where people lead a strenuous life", it would not relate to the thesis? The example of Diana's visit to Africa seems to show that Diana has learned something through her experience in helping other people. So obviously, the writer doesn't give an appropriate example here. But, still, there is a way to use the same example. By saying people can always learn, influenced or inspired by other people's behaviors, the writer then can describe the story of Diana's to indicate that schools, while certainly important, constitute only a relatively small part of education;learning from other people is an important way of education as well. The essay exhibits somewhat varied sentence structure with some flaws in mechanics, usage and grammar.

Suggestion to readers:

Ask yourself a question before you decide to use an example or show evidence: Does my example or evidence support my thesis strongly?

Topic 2: Can knowledge be a burden rather than a benefit?

Think carefully about the issue presented in the following excerpt and the assignment below.

> Knowledge is power. In agriculture, medicine, and industry, for example, knowledge has liberated us from hunger, disease, and tedious labor. Today, however, our knowledge has become so powerful that it is beyond our control. We know how to do many things, but we do not know where, when, or even whether this know-how should be used.

Assignment: Can knowledge be a burden rather than a benefit? Plan and write an essay in which you develop your point of view on this issue. Support your position with reasoning and examples taken from your reading, studies, experience, or observations.

Essay 1

Knowledge is power; it liberates us, enlightens us, allows us to grow and expand and better our conditions. Today, our knowledge of the world has grown immensely, and could be seen as "beyond our control" , and even a burden.

However, history shows us that while great knowledge can sometimes be a heavy burden, it always has outweighing benefits.

History is rife with examples of knowledge being a burden, but ultimately proving to be beneficial. For instance, Galileo, a 17th century astronomer and scientist, was arguably the greatest contributor to science of our time. His diligent research of our Earth and solar system led to groundbreaking discoveries that, at the time, were extremely controversial. Galileo was the first scientist, and person, to question the Church's statement that the Earth was the center of the solar system, and all other planets and the Sun revolved around it. He instead argued, and proved through research, that the Sun was the center of our galaxy, and Earth just another planet in its orbit. This knowledge was profound, enlightening, and powerful; it was also a great burden.

Galileo's theory was met with disbelief, outrage, and violent opposition; it was an extreme burden to him. The Church was furious at Galileo for disproving its teachings because at the time, the Church's word was law. Never before had its teachings been so scientifically and poignantly questioned. To think that the Earth wasn't the center around which all things revolved was a shocking and humbling fact that those so fervently set in their beliefs couldn't accept. Galileo was immediately attacked and interrogated because of his powerful knowledge. He was declared a heretic, and excommunicated from the Church. Galileo was a very religious man; this social and spiritual ostracizing broke him completely. Even still, he knew that although his knowledge was a heavy and painful burden, it was true, and would later benefit generations of scientists to come. Today, attribute Galileo's discoveries as some of the most important scientific findings of the common era.

Galileo's story is a historical example of powerful knowledge being a burden, but ultimately having extremely positive benefits. If it weren't for great minds constantly expanding our knowledge of the world, we would be a stagnant peoples, never moving forward and creating new and marvelous things. Knowledge truly is a tool that can change the world and although it may sometimes be inconvenient, it is the most powerful thing we have.

(Source: New SAT OG)

Essay Score: 6

Scoring Explanation

The essay effectively and insightfully develops the main idea that "while great knowledge can sometimes be a heavy burden, it always has outweighing benefits." Using the clearly appropriate example of "Galileo's story" to support the thesis, the essay demonstrates critical thinking. The essay is well organized and clearly focused as it describes the importance of "great minds constantly expanding our knowledge··· creating new and marvelous things." The response displays clear coherence and smooth progression of ideas. (Galileo's theory was met with disbelief, outrage, and violent opposition; it was an extreme burden to him··· Even still, he knew that although his knowledge was a heavy and painful burden, it was true, and would later benefit generations of scientists to come.) The essay also demonstrates skillful use of language, using a varied, accurate vocabulary.

Suggestion to readers:

Three examples don't guarantee you a score of 6 and one example doesn't lower you chance of scoring high. It is quality, not quantity that counts.

Essay 2

Whether knowledge is a burden or a benefit depends on the way it is used.

Without knowledge, our society could still stagnate in the state of no antidotes against poisons or diseases, no techniques to germinate industrialization and no progressive transportation to facilitate globalization.

However, there are always two sides of a coin. Some people deviate the original intention of knowledge and misuse it to jeopardize the entire world. Take the alarming global warming for example, geologists used their extensive knowledge to discover many available resources underground; then unexpectedly immoderate and unceasing excavation ensued; what's more, the fatal pollution has taken over what our fragile planet used to be. Little has anyone contemplated about the repercussions.

Another example to cite, chemists prostitute their knowledge to produce drugs or psychedelic, which lead to further debauchery, induce more severe social pathology and disintegrate the stability that is procured at enormous sacrifice.

The Internet, probably correlating most of us every day, is another double-edged application of knowledge. The Internet undoubtedly provides myriad materials for our daily lives and allows us to get wind of the latest news from all over the world, which, I believe, is the main reason for its invention. Nonetheless, aberrant people use it wrong way again. They abuse their knowledge to spread spurious information, vulgar calumny or explicit photos, which debilitates people's trust in the information shown on Internet. All the agonizing behavior culminates in the dissemination of computer viruses. Their selfishness has indeed cast a gloomy shadow over the Internet.

According to the above-mentioned, much of our knowledge incipiently brought positive effects on us, whereas the consequent development was just out of control.

A conclusion can be generalized from these facts-knowledge is indispensable for the advancement of our society, but it is our morality and epiphany of what knowledge really means that make knowledge reach its apogee rather than become a burden.

Essay Score: 4

Scoring Explanation

This essay takes a position that "whether knowledge is a burden or a benefit depends on the way it is used," and displays competent critical thinking in providing several adequate examples. For the SAT essay, however, the writer has to choose one side on an issue by responding "Yes" or "No" , and then argue for or against it. Another weakness is the choice of words. The writer throws so many big words into the essay, among which some of them are not used appropriately. Take "Some people deviate the original intention of knowledge" as an example, "deviate" is an intransitive verb when meaning "to stray especially from a standard, principle, or topic." If followed by an object, we need to add from after the word. Also, what is original intention of knowledge, anyway?

Suggestion to readers:

Choose one side on the topic and write in a reader-friendly way and make sure you know exactly the meaning of the "big" words when use them.

Section VII: Success and adversity

Topic 1: Can success be disastrous?

Think carefully about the issue presented in the following excerpt and the assignment below:

> The old saying, "Be careful what you wish for," may be an appropriate warning. The drive to achieve a particular goal can dangerously narrow one's life perspective and encourage the fantasy that success in one endeavor will solve all of life's difficulties. In fact, success can sometimes have unexpected consequences. Those who propel themselves toward the achievement of one goal often find that their lives are worse once "success" is achieved than they were before.

Assignment: Can success be disastrous? Plan and write an essay in which you develop your point of view on this issue. Support your position with reasoning and examples taken from your reading, studies, experience, or observations.

Essay 1

The fantasy that success brings seems endlessly sweet for the people who pursue the success. They believe success will bring everything they want and expect to have a wonderful life than ever. However, the obsession toward achieving a success can be very dangerous. I believed, once reached, success can be disastrous to the people.

Success can impair one's insight. Once one reaches the point that he desires for, he is indulged in fragile and transient paradise of success. Julius Caesar, for example, was a great war-hero of his time who achieved his dream of unifying the Rome and ruling the prosperous country. However, his leadership and keen insight evanesced throughout his glorified victory. As a result, he was killed by his own people including Brutus whom he considered as his own brother.

The Great Depression of 1929 also shows how people can be biased once they possessed their goals. At the time, the stock prices were at their zeniths and even the middle class poured their savings into the stock market, only few foreshadowed the ominous consequences. Although, those few warned people of catastrophe, people did not listen and even ridicule them for being "paranoid" . The success they achieved through the stock market absolutely blocked their thoughts from the great possibility of impending calamity.

What success gives seduces people and leads the unpleasant consequences. To enjoy the success, one should never reside on one side- its sweetness. The real success is accomplished when one realized the duration of success and move on to the next step. Otherwise, success is a disaster, not the fantasy everybody dreams of.

Essay Score: 3

Scoring Explanation

The essay demonstrates some critical thinking in developing a point of view (the obsession toward achieving a success can be very dangerous. I believed, once reached, success can be disastrous to the people). Offering two reasons, one from Julius Caesar and one from the Great Depression of 1929, the essay features some organization and coherence. However, these two reasons are thinly developed, with support consisting of general and at times unclear ideas. For example, the writer explains that "As a result, he was killed by his own people including Brutus whom he considered as his own brother" . The writer doesn't establish a direct and clear relationship between Caesar's success and his disastrous consequence and the description is against the fact. During that time, the Roman middle and lower classes, with whom Caesar was popular, became enraged a small group of aristocrats who finally decided to kill Caesar. So we cannot conclude that Caesar's success leads to his death, which logically doesn't make any sense. And it seems to say that Martin Luther King's death is due to his success in organizing non-violent movement against segregation and injustice in the American south or the assassination of Lincoln is because of Lincoln's success of being the President of the United States of America. What's more, "including Brutus whom he considered as his own brother" in the sentence is meaningless and doesn't support anything. The essay sometimes uses weak vocabulary and lacks variety in sentence structure.

Suggestion to readers:

Use competent critical thinking to offer stronger support for the position.

Essay 2

In life, everyone sets his or her own personal targets and if one day these objectives might be achieved, then this would be defined as success. Success is a beautiful feeling that comes after hard work and sacrifice but could it perhaps be disastrous? Success can lead people into danger by changing a person's personality and making one do something that is out of character.

Many a time people give up so much of their time and even their money just to accomplish their objective because they believe that if they are successful then it would make their life more exciting, and more meaningful. However this isn't always the case for athletes, businessmen and politicians who tend to become even thirstier for greater feats even after they have achieved their main goal. Diego Armanda Maradona was one who won the Football World Cup in 1986 only to become banned from football later on in his life due to drug abuse. Despite his empathic achievements, he wasn't satisfied and due to his advancing years he had to keep up with the enduring game by aiding his cause with performance enhancers.

Success could also lead someone to relax and forget about one's principles because that feeling of satisfaction, that success brings, was too big for one to handle. Irish football player, George Best, had won all that there was to win at the modest age of just 22. From this point on Best started to spend more time in pubs rather than on the training pitch, keeping fit. He was forced to retire at a relatively young age due to liver problems that came about with his drinking habits. Best had a tragic ending to his life when he did because of liver failure in his early 50's. He probably felt that he had achieved it all and wasn't able to look for other possible objectives to keep him going.

Businessmen also find that success could bring about greed, by them not being satisfied of their achievements, but they'd rather move on to bigger things, possibly even bend the rules and lose self dignity, but if that will reward them with more and greater success, then so be it.

One must realise that success is vital for living a meaningful life and one must always seek to achieve what one is able to do, but one must do so by maintaining dignity, one's principles and realising what is really important in life. Success doesn't necessarily come in the form of power or money but it could also be expressed in good deeds towards society.

Essay Score: 4

Scoring Explanation

This essay demonstrates adequate mastery in developing its point of view (Success can lead people into danger by changing a person's personality and making one do something that is out of character). The essay displays competent critical thinking in providing several adequate examples including football players Diego Armanda Maradona and George Best. However, one example from a politician's fact or a specific example about a businessman would make the argument more convincing. The essay is adequately organized and displays some progression of ideas. But the ending is problematic when stating "it could also be expressed in good deeds towards society" as doing good deeds has not been mentioned previously.

The essay also exhibits adequate facility in the use of language in spite of some mistakes in spelling and grammar as in "However this is not always the case for athletes (Correct: However this is not always the case for athletes)."

Suggestion to readers:

Use language more effectively and provide focused evidence relevant to the topic.

Topic 2: Is striving to achieve a goal always the best course of action, or should people give up if they are not making progress?

Think carefully about the issue presented in the following excerpt and the assignment below.

The history of human achievement is filled with stories of people who persevere, refusing to give up in the struggle to meet their goals. Artists and scientists, for instance, may struggle for years without any apparent progress or reward before they finally succeed. However, it is important to recognize that perseverance does not always yield beneficial results.

- Adapted from Robert H. Lauer and Jeanette C. Lauer, Watersheds

Assignment: Is striving to achieve a goal always the best course of action, or should people give up if they are not making progress? Plan and write an essay in which you develop your point of view on this issue. Support your position with reasoning and examples taken from your reading, studies, experience, or observations.

Essay 1

Everybody knows Einstein's quote: "Genius is 1% inspiration and 99% perspiration." Perseverance plays a very significant role in success. However, few people look at the more pessimistic side of the story; what if perseverance just doesn't get you anywhere?

It is important to recognize that failure is always a possibility, often one that happens more often than its neighbor across the street. As the saying goes: "There is a thin line between genius and insanity, likewise between a great idea, and a crazy one." Several hundred years ago, for example, people believed that the Earth was flat, which was proved wrong during the Renaissance. Even the most persistent could not push an idea that was no longer plausible, or even relevant, though many tried.

Perseverance is not just about getting through a hard time or "building character" , it is also about learning from previous mistakes. At the end, there is something to look back to, or something to take from, whether it be experience, self-esteem or a physical object. The Wright Brothers spend many years trial-and-erroring before achieving their first real flight. In the book Holes, Stanley Yelnats III spent many years trying to recycle old sneakers, but instead, invented a way to eliminate foot odor. J.K. Rowling's first book of the Harry Potter series was sent to 8 publishers before it was even considered. Emily Carr's paintings were not well-known until late in her career. In all of these cases, inventors, authors, artists, failure was possible and likely, because countless others have experienced it, stories we never hear about.

"Just keep walking; the darkness eventually disappears." There is always light at the end of the tunnel; it's just up to us to walk until we find it.

Essay Score: 6

Scoring Explanation

This outstanding essay insightfully and effectively develops the point of view that "Perseverance plays a very significant role in success." Using the clearly appropriate examples of a series of facts including the inventors Wright Brothers, the writer J.K. Rowling and the artist Emily Carr, the essay is well organized and clearly focused as it illustrates that striving to achieve a goal is always the best course of action. The response displays clear coherence and smooth progression of ideas. The essay also exhibits skillful use of language, using a varied, accurate, and apt vocabulary, and meaningful variety in sentence structure is evident. Quotes like "Genius is 1% inspiration and 99% perspiration" and "There is a thin line between genius and insanity, likewise between a great idea, and a crazy one" are also appropriated used in the essay. Demonstrating clear and consistent mastery, this essay, therefore, merits a score of 6.

Essay 2

A philosopher once said, "Success only ends when you decide to give up." This famous quote proved to be true over history. Although success is not usually achieved spontaneously, the perseverance people have in order to accomplish their dreams is truly admirable. William Golding and Ray Borque are two exemplars of continual determination acting as the keystone of their success.

William Golding was a powerful writer who had great influence over writing in the twentieth century. However, he struggled to gain recognition at the beginning of his career. His most famous book, Lork of the Flies, took over three years to publish. The manuscript was rejected not once, but then times. Luckily, Golding's determination never wavered with each rejection; he edited the transcript to make the story even more spellbinding. Finally, Golding's eleventh attempt was successful and Lord of the Flies soon became a world wide pheneomon. Had Golding. forgo his pursue to publish Lord of the Flies, he would not have become the respected Nobel lateurate he is today.

Ray Borque was an admirable hockey player in the national hockey league (NHL). Although he was the recipient of many trophies such as the Art Ross or Lady Byng, he was more remembered for his continuous fight for the Stanley Cup. By 2000, Borque became the longest NHL player with a cup drought. He had played over 1000 games but never managed to capture his dreams. Many people persuaded Borque to retire and hang up his skates, but Borque's perseverance shook off these comments and acted as an incentive for him to become a better player. Finally, Borque won the Stanley Cup that year. The moment he lifted and kissed the cup, the crowd gave him a standing ovation for his accomplishment of his dream. Borque is now a Hall of Famer who will always an inspiring model for younger generations.

Although struggles may impede the way to success, perseverance will always outlast these difficulties. William Golding and Ray Borque are two iconic examples whose success was made possible by their determination.

Essay Score: 5

Scoring Explanation

This essay demonstrates effective skill in responding to the task. The writer takes a position (Success only ends when you decide to give up." This famous quote proved to be true over history. Although success is not usually achieved spontaneously, the perseverance people have in order to accomplish their dreams is truly admirable.) and offers context for the discussion. Demonstrating strong critical thinking, the essay uses appropriate examples of William Golding and Ray

Borque to support its position. Well organized and focused, the essay exhibits coherence and progression of ideas, and facility in the use of language. However, the conclusion is weak, which is mere repetition of what is said in the previous parts and doesn't provide thoughtful commentary. There are also some grammatical errors such as "forgo his pursue to publish (correct: pursuit)" and "become the respected Nobel lateurate (correct: laureate)" .

Suggestion to readers:

Make your language more effectively and learn to write a powerful conclusion.

Essay 3

Although perseverance does not always yield beneficial results, I think people should always strive to achieve a goal instead of just giving up if no progress were made. The history of human achievement is filled with stories of people who preserved. It's unlikely that a person can succeed in achieving a goal without any struggle. And this applies to everyone. For example, in order for a scientist to get the answer to his research question, he or she will have to conduct numerous experiments. The experiments may contain errors or provide obstacle, but the scientists have to solve. It's through this process that a scientist learns. If people all gave up, the society will deteriorate because no technical, artistic or scientific improvements are made. Failure lead people to success. Nothing will be achieved if people gave up after their failed attempts.

Also, people learn from their mistakes. Giving up eliminates opportunitie for people can not only learn from books, but also experiences. I had a friend who was competing in a physic contest when he first finished his "mousetrap ship" , the mousetrap not only failed to trap anything, the force of the trap broke the ship apart. Instead of giving up, my friend analyzed the broken ship, and the film he took he was trying out the mouse trap. Step by step, he reconstructed his mousetrap ship.

He failed a second, a third time. It wasn't until the tenth time that he succeeded. Later on, he won the competition. The only thing he said to me was "It's through failures I learned. Never give up." Therefore, I think even if the outcomes of perseverance aren't always beneficial, the best course of action to achieve a goal is striving. If one doesn't try, how does one know that he or she can't succeed.

Essay Score: 4

Scoring Explanation

The essay develops a point of view on the issue and demonstrates competent critical thinking, using adequate examples and reasons to support its position.

Demonstrating some coherence and progression of ideas, the essay, however, is weakly organized as the introduction, discussion and conclusion are all unclear. It seems that the writer does have a lot to say, but doesn't organize them well. The writer demonstrates adequate ability with language, using a variety of sentence types and some appropriate word choice. Still, there are some errors in spelling.

Suggestion to readers:

Organization! Organization! Organization!

Essay 4

If we look back at the great achievements throughout this century, we can find a common factor which lead to these accomplishments, which is: effort. Just as Mark Twaiw had once said, "Don't follow the path but make our own and leave a trail." His statement clearly illustrates that we would remain stagnant unless we can strive to achieve our goals rather than merely following an already set course such as the process of schooling. However, during the periods when we are in school, we are often confronted by two pathways. One is to follow the path which is already paved down for us, that is without any effort because we are merely following the expectations. On the other hand, the second option is to pave our own way, that is to strive forward and change the direction at our sail to achieve our goals. Therefore, effort is an essential factor that can lead one to one's success. Examples such as historical achievements and modern accomplishment can best emphasize the need to thrive forward.

One historical event which already shows that striving to achieve a goal is often the best course of action, is that the building of Canadian national identity. Although in the mid-1800s, Canada was only a colony under the British Empire, Canadians wanted to follow their own path and together they worked tirelessly and diligently towards and independent nation. From this event, the common factor which led to the Canadian's success is the effort to move forward and to change their conventions. Therefore, it is evident that to achieve great goals the best course of action is often to strive forward.

Another example, unlike the first one, is a modern accomplishment. Barack Obama, the president of the United State battled through numerous contemptuous confrontations because of his race. He is the first African-American to become the president and it is evident that he did not achieve his goal with mere publicity nor money. He strove forward with his effort. In the end, the result is clear, he succeed and the key which lead to his success is the effort to go against the odds. Therefore, either from history or modern times, it is evident that great goals often need immense efforts and the notion to thrive forward rather than stay stagnant.

In a word, although we often can not change which country, family we are born either rich or poor, we can always change our life by making an effort to thrive forward and confront the odds and the conventions.

Essay Score: 3

Scoring Explanation

The essay demonstrates some critical thinking in developing a point of view. The position the essay takes is clear; however, the statement the essay makes is somewhat off the topic. As the topic is about if people's striving to achieve a goal always the best course of action, or people should give up if they are not making progress, in which, the point is supposed to be a question of "perseverance" . Should people persevere or should they give up in the struggle to meet their goals when making no progress? The essay, however, mostly explains about "effort" instead of perseverance. In the introduction, some statements are meaningless. For example, the quote "Don't follow the path but make your own and leave a trail," is irrelevant to the topic.

Offering two reasons, the essay features some organization and coherence. However, these reasons are thinly developed; with support consisting of general and at times unclear ideas. The essay doesn't explain how hard Canadians strive to achieve the goal.

It could have been better if the essay described some facts about obstacles people had been confronted but they didn't give up, instead, they strove forward and finally achieved the great goal.

The essay sometimes uses weak vocabulary. The repeatedly used word of "evident" would not merit the score. To achieve a higher score, the essay needs to use more competent critical thinking and improved language facility to offer stronger support for its position.

Suggestion to readers:

Always focus on the topic.

Topic 3: Is it more important to do work that one finds fulfilling or work that pays well?

Think carefully about the issue presented in the following excerpt and the assignment below.

Most human beings spend their lives doing work they hate and work that the world does not need. It is of prime importance that you learn early what you want to do and whether or not the world needs this service. The return from your work must be the satisfaction that work brings you and the world's need of that work. Income is not money, it is satisfaction; it is creation; it is beauty.

- Adapted from W.E.B. Du Bois, The Autobiography of W.E.B. Du Bois: A Soliloquy on Viewing My Life from the Last Decade of Its First Century

Assignment: Is it more important to do work that one finds fulfilling or work that pays well? Plan and write an essay in which you develop your point of view on this issue. Support your position with reasoning and examples taken from your reading, studies, experience, or observations.

Essay

It is much more important to do work that one finds fulfilling rather than work that pays well. Although some would argue that work that pays well is fulfilling, they are clearly mistaken because they fail to acknowledge that it is the satisfaction that comes from work that is more important than income. Two examples from my personal experiences serve as compelling evidence of this fact.

Volunteer work is an example of this idea. Last summer I had two jobs at once: a volunteer job, and a job with a set income. In my volunteer work at my local hospital I enjoyed my time transporting patients and talking to nurses. Regardless of the fact that I received no income for my work shifts (4 hours a day), I actually obtained satisfaction from helping the nurses with their paperwork and transporting patients out of the hospital. However, in my job at K-mart I received a decent pay of ten-dollars an hour, but nevertheless I spent my time there miserable to the point when I quit after three weeks. Although K-mart pays well for the average high school student, my heart was not into the work and therefore I decided to quit. Working at the cash register of K-mart felt like being locked in a room and forced to look at every item that people bought. What does this show? Income does not have more importance than the satisfaction a person gets from doing a job that he or she loves. It is better to follow your heart rather than let money corrupt it.

Another example of this is seen through my friend Benito. Benito's parents always wanted him to become a doctor, and reluctantly Benito agreed and went to Harvard medical school. However, his dream was always to become a writer. In college he spent his four years miserably because he complied with his parents belief that being a doctor provides a stable income along with some prestige. When he graduated medical school and started out as an intern he could no longer take it. He told his parents that he did not want to be a doctor and that he would write for the rest of his life. Although he did it late, he followed his heart. Today he does not make a lot of money writing but most importantly he is happy.

Indeed, it is more important to find work fulfilling, rather than work that pays well. These experiences from my life portray this to be true.

Essay Score: 4

Scoring Explanation

Demonstrating competent critical thinking, the essay develops a point of view on the issue that "It is much more important to do work that one finds fulfilling rather than work that pays well." The essay then uses examples of the writer's personal experiences and experience from his or her friend to support its position. Examples about the writer's satisfaction with a volunteer work and dissatisfaction with a job by which he or she earns money though explain that "it is more important to find work fulfilling, rather than work that pays well." However, both of the examples are from the personal experience would make argument less convincing.

The essay is generally organized and focused, demonstrating some coherence and progression of ideas. The essay exhibits adequate but inconsistent facility in the use of language and has some errors in grammar, usage and mechanics.

Suggestion to readers:

Don't pick two personal experience examples as evidence or reason. Remember the statement from the assignment: Support your position with reasoning and examples taken from your reading, studies, experience, or observation.

Section VIII: Making decisions

Topic 1: What two options are the most difficult to choose between?

Think carefully about the issue presented in the following excerpt and the assignment below.

Educator William Morris once said to parents of high school students, "the true test of a person's character lies in what he or she chooses to do when no one is looking." Others believe that character is constantly being formed and refined by the series of choices a person make during his or her lifetime. Yet it is often very challenging to decide between to options which seem equally valuable.

Assignment: What two options are the most difficult to choose between? In an essay, support your position by discussing an example or examples from literature, arts, science, technology, history, current events, or your own experience or observation.

Essay 1

Man has constantly been at odds with himself, often having to make difficult choices to resolve this inner conflict. The most challenging of these choices is that of deciding between society's rules and laws, and those of the self. The veracity of this claim is evidenced by Mark Twain's literary masterpiece, The Adventures of Huckleberry Finn, and Arthur Dimmesdale's plight in Nathaniel Hawthorne's The

Scarlet Letter.

The Adventures of Huckleberry Finn chronicles the journey of a young boy Huck and a runaway slave, Jim. The two spend a majority of the novel traveling down the Mississippi River, and throughout this trip, Twain provides a number of powerful messages. Through his narrative style, Twain excellently captures Huck's moral dilemma between returning Jim to the authorities, as society would mandate, and keeping Jim with him, as Huck feels is correct. Clearly, Huck's internal conflict here is fueled by a fundamental misunderstanding of whether society's or the self's values are higher. Twain shows here that the choice between these two sets of values is indeed the most difficult decision to make.

Not only is the difficulty of the choice between society's values and the individual's values, or the defense of each, seen in the modern novel, Huck Finn, but also in the novel The Scarlet Letter, by Nathaniel Hawthorne. In the novel, Hester Prynne, a woman living during the Puritan times of America's inception, has committed adultery with, unbeknownst to the townspeople, the Reverend Arthur Dimmesdale. She is being punished for her sin, primarily by having to wear a scarlet "A" on her chest, while Dimmesdale is not. Dimmesdale sees that if he confesses his sin, he will achieve moral reconciliation, but hesitates in doing so because such an action would undermine the very Puritan beliefs that the town was founded upon. Indeed, the difficulty of this choice drives him to near-insanity, and the reverent eventually dies from the psychological battle that rages in his mind. Hawthorne thereby shows us that the most difficult choice to make is truly that between society and the self.

All in all, it is clear that the toughest options to choose between are those of society's laws and values and individual ones, as is seen through the novels Huck Finn and The Scarlet Letter.

Essay Score: 5

Scoring Explanation

This essay demonstrates mastery in developing its point of view (The most challenging of these choices is that of deciding between society's rules and laws, and those of the self.) on the issue and demonstrates strong critical thinking. The examples, one from Mark Twain's The Adventures of Huckleberry Finn and one from Nathaniel Hawthorne's The Scarlet Letter, powerfully support the view. The first example describes Huck's internal conflict which is fueled by a fundamental misunderstanding of whether society's or the self's values is higher. The second one illustrates Dimmesdale's dilemma that he "sees that if he confesses his sin, he will achieve moral reconciliation, but hesitates in doing so because such an action would undermine the very Puritan beliefs that the town was founded upon··· the difficulty of this choice drives him to near-insanity···" By presenting the examples, this well-organized essay demonstrates progression of ideas and coherence. The essay exhibits facility in the use of language and variety in sentence structure. However, the conclusion, which is mere repetition of what has been stated before, makes the argument flat.

Suggestion to readers:

Avoid using needless repetition.

Essay 2

Choosing between practicality and morality when it comes to business and politics can be a major challenge. While the pragmatic side of our brains command us to choose the most practical and profitable option, the romantic side of our brain tells us to follow the moral norm.

When it comes to business, practicality versus morality remains a critical issue. Although industrialization creates profit, its effect on the environment is detrimental. Mining companies, in particular, struggle to make their decisions. Their massive production of numeral waste can sometimes outweigh their benefits. Due to the current punctuation on pollution, problems such as air pollution, oil spoil and deforestation can reveal a company's moral standards, which influence the company's reputation. When company executors make decisions, they should not only consider the benefits of being practical, but also measure the potential danger of being unethical towards the environment.

This struggle in decision making also apply to politicians. Barack Obama promised through his speeches that he has no intention of making any military actions against other nations, and that America would be a friend of each nation. He promised these because people believe they are morally correct. However, President Obama had to send $30,000$ soldiers to Afghanistan in order to maintain democracy, equality and freedom. Although such action was ideal and practical, Obama's honest reputation was diminished. The military action would also increase the number of casualty in Afghanistan. Therefore, it is guaranteed that this decision was a challenge for President Obama.

Practicality and morality pose a major problem for many individuals. When it comes to decision making, it is crucial that we balance these two factors. Even though morality should be weighted equality as heavy as practicality, successful individuals, such as Obama and company CEOs tend to favor practicality. Practicality being our idol might become our next focus.

Essay Score: 5

Scoring Explanation

This essay effectively develops the main idea (Choosing between practicality and morality when it comes to business and politics can be a major challenge) with clearly appropriate reasons and examples about businessmen's decisions between profits and environment issues and Obama's action when making military decisions. Demonstrating critical thinking, the essay is well organized and focused, and shows clear coherence and smooth progression of ideas. It is also generally free of most errors in grammar, usage and mechanics. However, to achieve a score of 6, the essay needs to use language more effectively as the writer keeps using the phrase "when it comes to···" to start a sentence, and demonstrates variety in sentence structure.

Suggestion to readers:

Check to see that you do not start sentences with the same words or phrases as repetition weakens the quality of your writing. Having a good vocabulary will help you avoid repetition

---

Topic 2: Are people best defined by what they do?

Think carefully about the issue presented in the following excerpt and the assignment below.

> People define themselves by work, by what they "do." When one person asks another, "What do you do?" the answer always refers to a job or pro-fession: "I'm a doctor, an accountant, a farmer." I've often wondered what would happen if we changed the question to, "Who are you?" or, "What kind of person are you" or even," What do you do for fun?
>
> - Adapted from Stephan Rechtschaffen, Time Shifting

Assignment

Are people best defined by what they do? Plan and write an essay in which you develop your point of view on this issue. Support your position with reasoning and examples taken from your reading, studies, experience, or observations.

Essay

People tirelessly go about spending their days worrying about putting on makeup, dealing with teachers, and impressing employers. To what purpose do we invest such a monumental amount of time and effort on these aspects of life? We decide to do so because it is an innate and congenial trait to mind what others think of us. We want to leave a brilliant impression on others. The next question is how. The best way to etch a good memory of who we are is to do things. From holistic aspects such as careers to minute details like table manners, we consciously try to impress. As we increasingly act out this role of a "good" person, we become that. As a result, we become what we decide to do.

Examing history of all cultures we will notice that all figures, recorded in documents that survived the decaying phenomenon that is driven by time, are prevailed to this day because of their accomplishments. Napoleon led a brilliant career as a general and an emperor, influencing the path of European politics. Alexander the Great carved out one of the largest empires in history. George Washington led Americans to precious freedom. All these individuals are studied and admired because they did great things in their lifetimes. We too are remembered, on a much less grandiose scale, by our actions.

People are aware of this truth in literature as well. In the play Macbeth, the thane Macbeth at the beginning fought fearlessly in the face of great adversary, and so he was regarded by all as a noble warrior worthy of praise. However, as he fell from grace and succumbed to dark desires, he began to do despicable things, such as murder. In effect, those once loyal to him turned away, leaving him alone in the dark. This shows not only do our actions create impressions, they can also warp preset ones.

People want to be loved. As a result, we do things to impress others. When others sitdown to categorized who we are, they base it on what we do. This phenomenon in various ways propells humanity forward. Because society supports "good" deeds, our pursuits to impress also drives society to progress positively, such as through science and civil improvements.

Essay Score: 6

Scoring Explanation

This essay effectively and insightfully develops the main idea (As we increasingly act out this role of a "good" person, we become that. As a result, we become what we decide to do) with clearly appropriate reasons and examples, demonstrating outstanding critical thinking. Well organized and focused, the essay shows clear coherence and smooth progression of ideas (Napoleon⋯Alexander the Great⋯George Washington⋯ All these individuals are studied and admired because they did great things in their lifetimes. We too are remembered, on a much less grandiose scale, by our actions). It also consistently displays skillful use of language and meaningful variety in sentence structure. (People tirelessly go about spending their days worrying about putting on makeup, dealing with teachers, and impressing employers. To what purpose do we invest such a monumental amount of time and effort on these aspects of life? We decide to do so because it is an innate and congenial trait to mind what others think of us. We want to leave a brilliant impression on others. The next question is how⋯) Although there are spelling errors as in "Examing (Correct: Examining) history of all cultures we will notice⋯" and "This phenomenon in various ways propells (Correct: propels) humanity forward," the essay is basically free of most errors in usage and mechanics. This outstanding essay exhibits clear and consistent mastery and earns a score of 6.

Suggestion to readers:

Although the essay receives the highest score of 6, it could have been better if the spelling errors were avoided. So if you still have time, you know what you have to do... right?

Section IX: Others

Topic 1: Does fame bring happiness, or are people who are not famous more likely to be happy?

Think carefully about the issue presented in the following excerpt and the assignment below.

> Most of us are convinced that fame brings happiness. Fame, it seems, is among the things people most desire. We believe that to be famous, for whatever reason, is to prove oneself and confirm that one matters in the world. And yet those who are already famous often complain of the terrible burden of fame. In fact, making the achievement of fame one's life goal involves commitments of time and effort that are usually wasted.
>
> - Adapted from Leszek Kolakowski, Freedom, Fame, Lying, and Betrayal: Essayson Everyday Life

Assignment: Does fame bring happiness, or are people who are not famous more likely to be happy? Plan and write an essay in which you develop your point of view on this issue. Support your position with reasoning and examples taken from your reading, studies, experience, or observations.

Essay

Fame does not necessarily bring happiness, because it depends upon how one defines happiness and contentness. In order to be happy one must first understand why they are seeking such fortune. Fame has its consequences and it is for this reason that it does not guarantee inevitable success and achievement. In Shakespeare's King Lear, the main character, the King sought to prove himself and confirm that he mattered. His fame ultimately led to his demise, and this matter of fact also applies to Melville's Captain Ahab from Moby Dick.

In King Lear, the King is depicted as a venerable public figure. He is well known throughout all of the land, however, his fame does not necessarily influence his contentness with life. His public image rather gives way to his vulnerability, and he ultimately becomes taken advantage of by his two self-gratification seeking daughters. Lear's unlimited surplus of goods, access to money, and entitlement to power influence his morose life. Lear's demise is the result of the terrible burdens of fame. His destruction occurs because he is so privileged and this relates to how fame is not a predecessor for enjoying life. His daughters sought to seek his fortune, and because of this matter he was forced to lead a mundane and melancholy life until he died.

In Moby Dick, Captain Ahab is perceived as an experienced and well to do ship captain. His fellow shipmates admire his tenacity and accomplishments, and this leads to this fame throughout his small sailing town in Boston. Throughout the story Ahab seeks to prove his worthiness by setting out to seek revenge upon the whale who ate his leg. Ahab is unable to take on the force of the whale and this ultimately leads to his destruction and untimely death. Ahab's perceived image and fame do not bring him happiness, because he constantly feels the need to prove himself. Ahab's desire and need to confirm that he is the ship captain that everyone makes him seem out to be influence his manic nature and ultimate discontent with life.

There is no definite way to ensure that fame brings about happiness, because it has so many consequences. Ahab and Lear are prime examples of how fame can evoke burdens in life, and lead to one's relative unhappiness and death. Both Ahab and Lear's commitments of time and effort were ultimately wasted, because their notoriety brought about their destruction and led to their unhappiness.

Essay Score: 5

Scoring Explanation

The essay effectively develops a point of view on the issue that "Fame does not necessarily bring happiness" and demonstrates strong critical thinking, generally using appropriate examples including the King, from Shakespeare's play King Lear and story of Captain Ahab from a novel in Moby Dick to support its position. The essay is well organized and focused, demonstrating coherence and progression of ideas. Using appropriate vocabulary, the essay exhibits facility in the use of language, and demonstrates variety in sentence structure. To achieve a higher score, this essay needs to demonstrate a slightly more skillful use of language to more insightfully and consistently develop the position.

Suggestion to readers:

Insightfulness, creativity and effectiveness.

Topic 2: Do incidents from the past continue to influence the present?

Think carefully about the issue presented in the following excerpt and the assignment below.

> Common sense suggest an obvious divisions between the past and present, between history and current events. In many cases, however, this boundary is not clear-cut because earlier events are not locked away in the past. Events from history remain alive through people's memories and through books, films, and other media. For both individuals and groups, incidents from the past continue to influence the present- sometimes positively and sometimes negatively.

Assignment: Do incidents from the past continue to influence the present? Plan and write an essay in which you develop your point of view on this issue. Support your position with reasoning and examples taken from your reading, studies, experience, or observations.

Essay

"You are what you remember." One of the traits that define being human is a person's congenital trait of remembering the past. What can more clearly distinguish the advanced race that is mankind, which has secured its dominance on the planet with a magnificent display of metropolitans of glass and space crafts of the future, from other forms of animal life, which are completely subject to the rule of nature. Humanity's ability to not only remember but to cognitively learn from wisdoms of the past ensures its limitless prosperity. We humans are constantly influenced by the past, because we know that this will propel us forward.

WWII left a devastating black mark on humanity's proud history. The world witnessed some of the most disdained atrocities manifest in senseless slaughter. Although the war eroded more than half a century ago, people of the present still remember. Once a year,people around the globe takes a moment to pay some respect to all soldiers. Friends and family will forever keep in mind that strife it caused when a soldier decided that a sacrifice was necessary to preserve the prosperity back home. World leaders now have recognized the backlash of such a war, and the UN was formed to deal with future violations against human rights. From the ashes of such a dark blow, humans took from it what they can to build a better future.

More directly influential, a man that went by Isaac Newton once SAT under a tree. When an apple fell, a spark hit him, and soon later, the laws of gravitation were formed. This knowledge proved crucial to scientists on their pursuits of invention. Planes, satellites and beyond all depend on Newton's theory. Without a doubt, his endeavors of the past have now been integrated to our everyday lives.

Memories define an individual, a culture, and the race. Humans embrace the past to brace for the future. From painful memories to marvelous discoveries, humans utilize them for future perils and good fortunes. The past will never cease to seep into our future.

Essay Score: 6

Scoring Explanation

This essay insightfully and effectively develops the point of the view that "Humanity's ability to not only remember but to cognitively learn from wisdoms of the past ensures its limitless prosperity." What's more, in the introductory paragraph, the writer appropriately and reasonably points out that "We humans are constantly influenced by the past, because we know that this will propel us forward," indicating a strong relationship between past, present and the future. By explaining what people of today have learned through the WWII and what people will do to deal with future violations against human rights, and the benefits Newton's theory has brought to scientists and the world of the present, the writer demonstrates outstanding critical thinking. The essay also displays smooth progression of ideas and clear coherence.

The essay exhibits skillful use of language, using a varied, accurate and apt vocabulary (WWII left a devastating black mark on humanity's proud history. The world witnessed some of the most disdained atrocities manifest in senseless slaughter⋯ Memories define an individual, a culture, and the race. Humans embrace the past to brace for the future).

Overall, this excellent essay demonstrates clear and consistent mastery, and therefore, receives the highest score of 6.

Suggestion to readers:

Read, think, and write.

S.A.T **Chapter VI**

Example sources for SAT

　　獲取 SAT 高分成績的關鍵在於論證。充分的論證素材，可以為論點提供強有力的事實依據。論點是否站得住腳，全靠論證做支撐。然而，如此重要的作文構成部分，恰恰是很多考生寫作中最薄弱的一個環節。面對題目，很多人往往有做「無米之炊」之感，立場確定了，觀點明確了，但是，用什麼論證素材來支持自己的觀點呢？如果題目是關於成功與失敗的，你的腦海裡是不是只浮現愛迪生一個人的名字？如果話題是關於鍥而不捨的精神，你是不是想到的還是愛迪生？當然，使用愛迪生做例證邏輯上並沒有錯誤，但是當你和很多人都在引用同一人物做例證時，這個例證素材已經沒有任何新意可言了。評分人會認為，你的邏輯雖然沒有錯誤，但是你的知識儲存量是有限的。同樣的上述兩個話題，用身患癌症卻不懼病魔最終取得環法自行車賽冠軍的阿姆斯壯做例證豈不更好。因此，為豐富學生論據資源，本章按寓言、人生哲理、歷史文獻、名人演講、人物分類，彙集了各種寫作論證素材。學生亦可依此拓展或建立個人素材資料。擁有了充分而詳盡的例證素材庫，考試時，學生才可做到從容面對，才思雋永，筆下生花。

　　One of the most misunderstood parts of the SATis the essay and one of the most difficult parts of the essay is how to show your ability to write a good response to a topic with appropriate and reasonable examples in only 25 minutes. Yet, if you plan, prepare and practice properly it will be the easiest part of the whole test. So, read the following stories and they will give you some clue of idea brainstorming.

　　Take Rousseau's story as an example, whose ideas about education have profoundly influenced modern educational theory. He minimizes the importance of book learning, and recommends that a child's emotions should be educated before his reason. He placed a special emphasis on learning by experience. The theory about learning from Rousseau, therefore, could be illustrated as an example to respond to the prompt that "Is education primarily the result of influences other than school? (January, 2007)"

Following is only for reference. You need to read more and while reading, don't forget "thinking" .

Section I: Law of life

Buddha's teaching

- Everything is impermanent and changes.
- Give up what is wrong and evil.
- Undertake what is good.
- Abandon thoughts that have to do with bringing suffering to any conscious being; cultivate thoughts that are of loving kindness, that are based on caring for others' suffering, and sympathetic joy in others' happiness.
- Abstain from telling lies.
- Abstain from talk that brings harm or discredit to others or talk that creates hatred or disharmony between individuals and groups.
- Abstain from harsh, rude, impolite, malicious, or abusive language.
- Abstain from harsh speech-practice kindly speech.
- Abstain from frivolous speech-practice meaningful speech.
- Abstain from slanderous speech-practice harmonious speech.
- Speak the truth if it is useful and timely. Practice only necessary speech. Let your speech be filled with loving kindness. Speak that which alleviates suffering.

Three fables

1. The ant works hard in the withering heat all summer long, building his house and laying up supplies for the winter. The grasshopper thinks the ant is a fool and laughs and dances and plays the summer away. Come winter, the ant is warm and well fed. The grasshopper has no food or shelter, so he dies out in the cold.

Moral:

Work hard and take responsibility for yourself.

---

2. A Hare one day ridiculed the short feet and slow pace of the Tortoise. The latter, laughing, said: "Though you be swift as the wind, I will beat you in a race." The Hare, deeming her assertion to be simply impossible, assented to the proposal; and they agreed that the Fox should choose the course, and fix the goal. On the day appointed for the race they started together. The Tortoise never for a moment stopped, but went on with a slow but steady pace straight to the end of the course. The Hare, trusting to his native swiftness, cared little about the race, and lying down by the wayside, fell fast asleep. At last waking up, and moving as fast as he could, he saw the Tortoise had reached the goal, and was comfortably dozing after her fatigue.

Moral:

Never give up.

---

3. A crow was sitting on a branch of a tree with a piece of cheese in her beak when a Fox observed her and set his wits to work to discover some way of getting the cheese. Coming and standing under the tree he looked up and said, "What a noble bird I see above me! Her beauty is without equal, the hue of her plumage exquisite. If only her voice is as sweet as her looks are fair, she ought without doubt to be Queen of the Birds." The Crow was hugely flattered by this, and just to show

the Fox that she could sing she gave a loud caw. Down came the cheese and the Fox, snatching it up, said, "You have a voice, madam, I see: what you want is wits." (Source: Aesop's Fables)

Moral:

Don't trust flatters.

What you should know about life

• Life is not fair, get used to it.

• The world won't care about your self-esteem. The world will expect you to accomplish something BEFORE you feel good about yourself.

• Flipping burgers is not beneath your dignity. Your grandparents had a different word for burger-flipping; they called it opportunity.

• Open your arms to change, but don't let go of your values.

• Life is not divided into semesters. You don't get summers off and very few employers are interested in helping you find yourself. Do that on your own time.

Section II: Historical documents and speeches

United States Declaration of Independence (Adopted in Congress 4 July 1776)

We hold these truths to be self-evident, that all men are created equal, that they are endowed by their Creator with certain unalienable rights, that among these are life, liberty and the pursuit of happiness. That to secure these rights, governments are instituted among men, deriving their just powers from the consent of the governed. That whenever any form of government becomes destructive to these ends, it is the right of the people to alter or to abolish it, and to institute new government, laying its foundation on such principles and organizing its powers in such form, as to them shall seem most likely to effect their safety and happiness. Prudence, indeed, will dictate that governments long established should not be changed for light and transient causes; and accordingly all experience hath shown that mankind are more disposed to suffer, while evils are sufferable, than to right themselves by abolishing the forms to which they are accustomed. But when a long train of abuses and usurpations, pursuing invariably the same object evinces a design to reduce them under absolute despotism, it is their right, it is their duty, to throw off such government, and to provide new guards for their future security. Such has been the patient sufferance of these colonies; and such is now the necessity which constrains them to alter their former systems of government. The history of the present King of Great Britain is a history of repeated injuries and usurpations, all having in direct object the establishment of an absolute tyranny over these states. To prove this, let facts be submitted to a candid world.

He has refused his assent to laws, the most wholesome and necessary for the public good.

He has forbidden his governors to pass laws of immediate and pressing importance, unless suspended in their operation till his assent should be obtained; and when so suspended, he has utterly neglected to attend to them.He has refused to pass other laws for the accommodation of large districts of people, unless those people would relinquish the right of representation in the legislature, a right inestimable to them and formidable to tyrants only.

He has called together legislative bodies at places unusual, uncomfortable, and distant from the depository of their public records, for the sole purpose of fatiguing them into compliance with his measures.

He has dissolved representative houses repeatedly, for opposing with manly firmness his invasions on the rights of the people.

He has refused for a long time, after such dissolutions, to cause others to be elected; whereby the legislative powers, incapable of annihilation, have returned to the people at large for their exercise; the state remaining in the meantime exposed to all the dangers of invasion from without, and convulsions within.

He has endeavored to prevent the population of these states; for that purpose obstructing the laws for naturalization of foreigners; refusing to pass others to encourage their migration hither, and raising the conditions of new appropriations of lands.

He has obstructed the administration of justice, by refusing his assent to laws for establishing judiciary powers.

He has made judges dependent on his will alone, for the tenure of their offices, and the amount and payment of their salaries.

He has erected a multitude of new offices, and sent hither swarms of officers to harass our people, and eat out their substance.

He has kept among us, in times of peace, standing armies without the consent of our legislature.

He has affected to render the military independent of and superior to civil power.

He has combined with others to subject us to a jurisdiction foreign to our constitution, and unacknowledged by our laws; giving his assent to their acts of pretended legislation:

> For quartering large bodies of armed troops among us;
>
> For protecting them, by mock trial, from punishment for any murders which they should commit on the inhabitants of these states;
>
> For cutting off our trade with all parts of the world;
>
> For imposing taxes on us without our consent;
>
> For depriving us in many cases, of the benefits of trial by jury;
>
> For transporting us beyond seas to be tried for pretended offenses;
>
> For abolishing the free system of English laws in a neighboring province, establishing therein an arbitrary government, and enlarging its boundaries so as tor ender it at once an example and fit instrument for introducing the same absolute rule in these colonies:

For taking away our charters, abolishing our most valuable laws, and altering fundamentally the forms of our governments;

For suspending our own legislatures, and declaring themselves invested with power to legislate for us in all cases whatsoever.

He has abdicated government here, by declaring us out of his protection and waging war against us.

He has plundered our seas, ravaged our coasts, burned our towns, and destroyed the lives of our people.

He is at this time transporting large armies of foreign mercenaries to complete the works of death, desolation and tyranny, already begun with circumstances of cruelty and perfidy scarcely paralleled in the most barbarous ages, and totally unworthy the head of a civilized nation.

He has constrained our fellow citizens taken captive on the high seas to bear arms against their country, to become the executioners of their friends and brethren, or to fall themselves by their hands.

He has excited domestic insurrections amongst us, and has endeavored to bring on the inhabitants of our frontiers, the merciless Indian savages, whose known rule of warfare, is undistinguished destruction of all ages, sexes and conditions.

In every stage of these oppressions we have petitioned for redress in the most humble terms: our repeated petitions have been answered only by repeated injury. A prince, whose character is thus marked by every act which may define a tyrant, is unfit to be the ruler of a free people.

Nor have we been wanting in attention to our British brethren. We have warned them from time to time of attempts by their legislature to extend an unwarrantable jurisdiction over us. We have reminded them of the circumstances of our emigration and settlement here. We have appealed to their native justice and magnanimity, and we have conjured them by the ties of our common kindred to disavow these usurpations, which, would inevitably interrupt our connections and correspondence. We must, therefore, acquiesce in the necessity, which denounces our separation, and hold them, as we hold the rest of mankind, enemies in war, in peace friends.

We, therefore, the representatives of the United States of America, in General Congress, assembled, appealing to the Supreme Judge of the world for the rectitude of our intentions, do, in the name, and by the authority of the good people of these colonies, solemnly publish and declare, that these united colonies are, and of right ought to be free and independent states; that they are absolved from all allegiance to the British Crown, and that all political connection between them and the state of Great Britain, is and ought to be totally dissolved; and that as free and independent states, they have full power to levy war, conclude peace, contract alliances, establish commerce, and to do all other acts and things which independent states may of right do. And for the support of this declaration, with a firm reliance on the protection of Divine Providence, we mutually pledge to each other our lives, our fortunes and our sacred honor.

Key words: equal

The Gettysburg Address (Nov. 19, 1863)

(The Gettysburg Address is a speech by U.S. President Abraham Lincoln and is one of the best-known speeches in United States history. It was delivered by Lincoln during the American Civil War, on the afternoon of Thursday, November 19, 1863, at the dedication of the Soldiers' National Cemetery in Gettysburg, Pennsylvania, four and a half months after the Union armies defeated those of the Confederacy at the decisive Battle of Gettysburg.)

Shortly after Everett's well-received remarks, Lincoln spoke for two or three minutes. Lincoln's "few appropriate remarks" summarized the war in ten sentences.

Despite the historical significance of Lincoln's speech, modern scholars disagree as to its exact wording, and contemporary transcriptions published in newspaper accounts of the event and even handwritten copies by Lincoln himself differ in their wording, punctuation, and structure. Of these versions, the Bliss version, written well after the speech as a favor for a friend, is viewed by many as the standard text. Its text differs, however, from the written versions prepared by Lincoln before and after his speech. It is the only version to which Lincoln affixed his signature, and the last he is known to have written.

"Four score and seven years ago our fathers brought forth on this continent a new nation, conceived in liberty, and dedicated to the proposition that all men are created equal.

"Now we are engaged in a great civil war, testing whether that nation, or any nation, so conceived and so dedicated, can long endure. We are met on a great battle-field of that war. We have come to dedicate a portion of that field, as a final resting place for those who here gave their lives that that nation might live. It is altogether fitting and proper that we should do this.

"But, in a larger sense, we can not dedicate, we can not consecrate, we can not hallow this ground. The brave men, living and dead, who struggled here, have consecrated it, far above our poor power to add or detract. The world will little note, nor long remember what we say here, but it can never forget what they did here. It is for us the living, rather, to be dedicated here to the unfinished work which they who fought here have thus far so nobly advanced. It is rather for us to be here dedicated to the great task remaining before us-that from these honored dead we take increased devotion to that cause for which they gave the last full measure of devotion-that we here highly resolve that these dead shall not have died in vain-that this nation, under God, shall have a new birth of freedom-and that government of the people, by the people, for the people, shall not perish from the earth."

Key words: dedicate, freedom

I have a Dream by Martin Luther King, Jr. (August 28, 1963)

(Delivered on the steps at the Lincoln Memorial in Washington D.C. on August 28, 1963)

Five score years ago, a great American, in whose symbolic shadow we stand signed the Emancipation Proclamation. This momentous decree came as a great beacon light of hope to millions of Negro slaves who had been seared in the flames of withering injustice. It came as a joyous daybreak to end the long night of captivity.

But one hundred years later, we must face the tragic fact that the Negro is still not free. One hundred years later, the life of the Negro is still sadly crippled by the manacles of segregation and the chains of discrimination. One hundred years later, the Negro lives on a lonely island of poverty in the midst of a vast ocean of material prosperity. One hundred years later, the Negro is still languishing in the corners of American society and finds himself an exile in his own land. So we have come here today to dramatize an appalling condition.

In a sense we have come to our nation's capital to cash a check. When the architects of our republic wrote the magnificent words of the Constitution and the declaration of Independence, they were signing a promissory note to which every American was to fall heir. This note was a promise that all men would be guaranteed the inalienable rights of life, liberty, and the pursuit of happiness.

It is obvious today that America has defaulted on this promissory note insofar as her citizens of color are concerned. Instead of honoring this sacred obligation, America has given the Negro people a bad check which has come back marked "insufficient funds" .But we refuse to believe that the bank of justice is bankrupt. We refuse to believe that there are insufficient funds in the great vaults of opportunity of this nation. So we have come to cash this check-a check that will give us upon demand the riches of freedom and the security of justice. We have also come to this hallowed spot to remind America of the fierce urgency of now. This is no time to engage in the luxury of cooling off or to take the tranquilizing drug of gradualism. Now is the time to rise from the dark and desolate valley of segregation to the sunlit path of racial justice. Now is the time to open the doors of opportunity to all of God's children. Now is the time to lift our nation from the quicksands of racial injustice to the solid rock of brotherhood.

It would be fatal for the nation to overlook the urgency of the moment and to underestimate the determination of the Negro. This sweltering summer of the Negro's legitimate discontent will not pass until there is an invigorating autumn of freedom and equality. Nineteen sixty-three is not an end, but a beginning. Those who hope that the Negro needed to blow off steam and will now be content will have a rude awakening if the nation returns to business as usual. There will be neither rest nor tranquility in America until the Negro is granted his citizenship rights. The whirlwinds of revolt will continue to shake the foundations of our nation until the bright day of justice emerges.

But there is something that I must say to my people who stand on the warm threshold which leads into the palace of justice. In the process of gaining our rightful place we must not be guilty of wrongful deeds. Let us not seek to satisfy our thirst for freedom by drinking from the cup of bitterness and hatred.

We must forever conduct our struggle on the high plane of dignity and discipline. We must not allow our creative protest to degenerate into physical violence. Again and again we must rise to the majestic heights of meeting physical force with soul force. The marvelous new militancy which has engulfed the Negro community must not lead us to distrust of all white people, for many of our white brothers, as evidenced by their presence here today, have come to realize that their destiny is tied up with our destiny and their freedom is inextricably bound to our freedom. We cannot walk alone.

And as we walk, we must make the pledge that we shall march ahead. We cannot turn back. There are those who are asking the devotees of civil rights, "When will you be satisfied?" We can never be satisfied as long as our bodies, heavy with the fatigue of travel, cannot gain lodging in the motels of the highways and the hotels of the cities. We cannot be satisfied as long as the Negro's basic mobility is from a smaller ghetto to a larger one. We can never be satisfied as long as a Negro in Mississippi cannot vote and a Negro in New York believes he has nothing for which to vote. No, no, we are not satisfied, and we will not be satisfied until justice rolls down like waters and righteousness like a mighty stream.

I am not unmindful that some of you have come here out of great trials and tribulations. Some of you have come fresh from narrow cells. Some of you have come from areas where your quest for freedom left you battered by the storms of persecution and staggered by the winds of police brutality. You have been the veterans of creative suffering. Continue to work with the faith that unearned suffering is redemptive.

Go back to Mississippi, go back to Alabama, go back to Georgia, go back to Louisiana, go back to the slums and ghettos of our northern cities, knowing that somehow this situation can and will be changed. Let us not wallow in the valley of despair.

I say to you today, my friends, that in spite of the difficulties and frustrations of the moment, I still have a dream. It is a dream deeply rooted in the American dream.

I have a dream that one day this nation will rise up and live out the true meaning of its creed: "We hold these truths to be self-evident: that all men are created equal."

I have a dream that one day on the red hills of Georgia the sons of former slaves and the sons of former slaveowners will be able to sit down together at a table of brotherhood.

I have a dream that one day even the state of Mississippi, a desert state, sweltering with the heat of injustice and oppression, will be transformed into an oasis of freedom and justice.

I have a dream that my four children will one day live in a nation where they will not be judged by the color of their skin but by the content of their character.

I have a dream today.

I have a dream that one day the state of Alabama, whose governor's lips are presently dripping with the words of interposition and nullification, will be transformed into a situation where little black boys and black girls will be able to join hands with little white boys and white girls and walk together as sisters and brothers.

I have a dream today.

I have a dream that one day every valley shall be exalted, every hill and mountain shall be made low, the rough places will be made plain, and the crooked places will be made straight, and the glory of the Lord shall be revealed, and all flesh shall see it together.

This is our hope. This is the faith with which I return to the South. With this faith we will be able to hew out of the mountain of despair a stone of hope. With this faith we will be able to transform the jangling discords of our nation into a beautiful symphony of brotherhood. With this faith we will be able to work together, to pray together, to struggle together, to go to jail together, to stand up for freedom together, knowing that we will be free one day.

This will be the day when all of God's children will be able to sing with a new meaning,"My country, 'tis of thee, sweet land of liberty, of thee I sing. Land where my fathers died, land of the pilgrim's pride, from every mountainside, let freedom ring."

And if America is to be a great nation this must become true. So let freedom ring from the prodigious hilltops of New Hampshire. Let freedom ring from the mighty mountains of New York. Let freedom ring from the heightening Alleghenies of Pennsylvania!

Let freedom ring from the snowcapped Rockies of Colorado!

Let freedom ring from the curvaceous peaks of California!

But not only that; let freedom ring from Stone Mountain of Georgia!

Let freedom ring from Lookout Mountain of Tennessee!

Let freedom ring from every hill and every molehill of Mississippi. From every mountainside, let freedom ring.

When we let freedom ring, when we let it ring from every village and every hamlet, from every state and every city, we will be able to speed up that day when all of God's children, black men and white men, Jews and Gentiles, Protestants and

Catholics, will be able to join hands and sing in the words of the old Negro spiritual, "Free at last! free at last! Thank God Almighty, we are free at last!"

Key words: rights of life, liberty, the pursuit of happiness

Blood, Sweat, and Tears, by Winston Churchill (May 13, 1940)

(Upon his very first entrance into the House of Commons as Britain's new Prime Minister on May 13, 1940, Winston Churchill only received a lukewarm reception from the assembly, while at his side, outgoing Prime Minister Neville Chamberlain was heartily cheered. Churchill then made this brief statement, which became one of the greatest calls-to-arms ever uttered. It came at the beginning of World War II when the armies of Adolf Hitler were roaring across Europe, seemingly unstoppable, conquering country after country for Nazi Germany, and when the survival of Britain itself seemed quite uncertain.)

On Friday evening last I received from His Majesty the mission to form a new administration. It was the evident will of Parliament and the nation that this should be conceived on the broadest possible basis and that it should include all parties. I have already completed the most important part of this task.

A war cabinet has been formed of five members, representing, with the Labour, Opposition, and Liberals, the unity of the nation. It was necessary that this should be done in one single day on account of the extreme urgency and rigor of events.

…

I now invite the House by a resolution to record its approval of the steps taken and declare its confidence in the new government.

The resolution

"That this House welcomes the formation of a government representing the united and inflexible resolve of the nation to prosecute the war with Germany to a victorious conclusion."

To form an administration of this scale and complexity is a serious undertaking in itself. But we are in the preliminary phase of one of the greatest battles in history. We are in action at many other points-in Norway and in Holland-and we have to be prepared in the Mediterranean. The air battle is continuing, and many preparations have to be made here at home.

In this crisis I think I may be pardoned if I do not address the House at any length today, and I hope that any of my friends and colleagues or former colleagues who are affected by the political reconstruction will make all allowances for any lack of ceremony with which it has been necessary to act.

I say to the House as I said to ministers who have joined this government, I have nothing to offer but blood, toil, tears, and sweat. We have before us an ordeal of the most grievous kind. We have before us many, many months of struggle and suffering.

You ask, what is our policy? I say it is to wage war by land, sea, and air. War with all our might and with all the strength God has given us, and to wage war against a monstrous tyranny never surpassed in the dark and lamentable catalogue of human crime. That is our policy.

You ask, what is our aim? I can answer in one word. It is victory. Victory at all costs-Victory in spite of all terrors-Victory, however long and hard the road may be, for without victory there is no survival.

Let that be realized. No survival for the British Empire, no survival for all that the British Empire has stood for, no survival for the urge, the impulse of the ages, that mankind shall move forward toward his goal.

I take up my task in buoyancy and hope. I feel sure that our cause will not be suffered to fail among men. I feel entitled at this juncture, at this time, to claim the aid of all and to say, "Come then, let us go forward together with our united strength."

Key words: blood, toil, tears, sweat, ordeal, struggle and suffering, and strength

---

William Faulkner on accepting Nobel Prize in Literature (December 10, 1950)

(William Faulkner was one of America's finest writers during the 20th century. He was born in New Albany, Mississippi. As a boy, his family moved to Oxford, Miss., the little town that became the setting for much of his beloved fiction. He created endearing characters in classic works such as: The Sound and the Fury, As I Lay Dying, Sanctuary, These Thirteen and Light in August. In 1949, he was awarded the Nobel Prize in Literature, during a time of worldwide fear over the possibility of atomic warfare. In this acceptance speech, he addresses those fears as they might impact young writers and reminds them of their duty.)

I feel that this award was not made to me as a man, but to my work-life's work in the agony and sweat of the human spirit, not for glory and least of all for profit, but to create out of the materials of the human spirit something which did not exist before. So this award is only mine in trust. It will not be difficult to find a dedication for the money part of it commensurate with the purpose and significance of its origin. But I would like to do the same with the acclaim too, by using this moment as a pinnacle from which I might be listened to by the young men and women already dedicated to the same anguish and travail, among whom is already that one who will some day stand where I am standing.

Our tragedy today is a general and universal physical fear so long sustained by now that we can even bear it. There are no longer problems of the spirit. There is only the question: When will I be blown up? Because of this, the young man or woman writing today has forgotten the problems of the human heart in conflict with itself which alone can make good writing because only that is worth writing about, worth the agony and the sweat.

He must learn them again. He must teach himself that the basest of all things is to be afraid; and, teaching himself that, forget it forever, leaving no room in his workshop for anything but the old verities and truths of the heart, the universal truths lacking which any story is ephemeral and doomed- love and honor and pity and pride and compassion and sacrifice. Until he does so, he labors under a curse.

He writes not of love but of lust, of defeats in which nobody loses anything of value, of victories without hope and, worst of all, without pity or compassion. His griefs grieve on no universal bones, leaving no scars. He writes not of the heart but of the glands.

Until he learns these things, he will write as though he stood among and watched the end of man. I decline to accept the end of man. It is easy enough to say that man is immortal simply because he will endure: that when the last ding-dong of doom has clanged and faded from the last worthless rock hanging tideless in the last red and dying evening, that even then there will still be one more sound: that of his puny inexhaustible voice, still talking. I refuse to accept this. I believe that man will not merely endure: he will prevail. He is immortal, not because he alone among creatures has an inexhaustible voice, but because he has a soul, a spirit capable of compassion and sacrifice and endurance. The poet's, the writer's, duty is to write about these things. It is his privilege to help man endure by lifting his heart, by reminding him of the courage and honor and hope and pride and compassion and pity and sacrifice which have been the glory of his past. The poet's voice need not merely be the record of man, it can be one of the props, the pillars to help him endure and prevail.

Key words: fear, agony, human spirit

Section III: Philosophers and thinkers

Laozi

Author of "Daodejing" , Laozi was one of the most distinguished philosophers of ancient China. The influence of the "Daodejing" , also translated as "The Laozi" , on Chinese culture is deep and pervasive. It explains the "Dao" or "Tao" and how it exists in the expression of "de" (virtue), through what he calls nature and "wu wei" (without doing anything). In other words, according to Laozi, humans' many unnatural actions cause the imbalance of the nature.

The "Daodejing" is written for leading the human beings to a return to their natural state. Laozi provides humans with a way of return, which is to free from unlimited desires and seek the natural and calm state of "wu wei". He emphasizes that "wu wei", seemingly meaning "without doing anything" and "non-action", is a word to explain "nature", which is the source all the values and ideologies originate from. In contrast to egoistial action, the term, "wu wei", indicates that simplicity and humility are vital virtues to every one. On a broader world issue level, it implies that human beings should cherish what they already have and keep the world in peace.

Laozi was an "axial" philosopher whose insight helps shape the course of human development. Phrases from the "Daodejing" such as "governing a large country is like cooking a small fish" have found their way into Western political rhetoric.

Key words: wu wei, simplicity, peace

Reference(s):

1. Karl Jaspers, Anaximander, Heraclitus, Parmenides, Plotinus, Lao-tzu, Nagarjuna. From The Great Philosophers, Vol. 2, The Original Thinkers. Ed. Hannah Arendt; trans. Ralph Manheim.

Confucius (551 BC-479 BC)

Kong Qiu, also known as Confucius or Kongzi, was a thinker, political figure, educator, and founder of the Ru School of Chinese thought. His teachings, preserved in the Lunyu, or Analects, emphasized personal and governmental morality, correctness of social relationships, justice and sincerity.

Confucius' social philosophy largely revolves around the concept of ren, "compassion" or "loving others". Those who have cultivated ren are "simple in manner and slow of speech". For Confucius, such concern for others is demonstrated through the practice of forms of the Golden Rule: "Never impose on others what you would not choose for yourself."

"Zi gong, a disciple of Confucius, once asked: 'Is there a word that could guide a person throughout his or her life?'

"Confucius said: 'How about shu (reciprocity): never impose on others what you would not choose for yourself?' "

Confucius also regards familial loyalty, devotion to parents and older siblings as a basis for an ideal govenment.

Key words: ren (loving others)

Reference(s):

1. Confucius, Stanford Encyclopedia of Philosophy
2. Analects XV.24, trans. David Hinton

Socrates (469 BC-399 BC)

In his use of critical reasoning, by his unwavering commitment to truth, and throughthe vivid example of his own life, the Greek logician Socrates was an important formative influence on Plato and set the standard for all subsequent Western philosophy.

Deservedly styled a philosopher, he neither secluded himself for study, nor opened a school for the regular instruction of pupils. He disclaimed the appellation of teacher; his practice was to converse. Early in the morning he frequented the public walks, the gymnasia for bodily training, and the school where youths were receiving instruction; he was to be seen at the market place at the hour when it was most crowded, among the booths and tables where goods were exposed for sale. His whole day was usually spent in this public manner. He talked with any one, young or old, rich or poor, who sought to address him, and in the hearing of all who stood by. As it was engaging, curious, and instructive to hear, certain persons made it their habit to attend him in public as companions and listeners.

However, some parents were displeased with his influence on their children, and his earlier association with opponents of the democratic regime had already made him a controversial political figure. An Athenian jury found charges-corrupting the youth and interfering with the religion of the city-upon which to convict Socrates, and they sentenced him to death in 399 B.C. Socrates accepted his death sentence when most thought he would simply leave Athens, as he felt he could not run away from or go against the will of his community.

Socrates' views on philosophy are shown through the dialogues of his student Plato. According to the dialogues, Socrates believed destroying the illusion that we already comprehend the world perfectly and accepting the fact of our own ignorance are important steps toward our acquisition of genuine knowledge.

He also emphasized people should focus on self-development rather than the pursuit of material wealth. He always invited others to concentrate more on friendships and a sense of true community, for Socrates felt this was the best way for people to grow together as a populace. Socrates stressed that "virtue was the most valuable of all possessions; the ideal life was spent in search of the good. Truth lies beneath the shadows of existence, and it is the job of the philosopher to show the rest how little they really know."

As one recent commentator has put it, plato, the idealist, offers "an idol, a master figure, for philosophy. A saint, a prophet of the 'Sun-God', a teacher condemned for his teachings as a heretic."

Key words: virtue, knowledge

Reference(s):

1. Plato, The Last Days of Socrates (1995), Hugh Tredennick (ed)

Friedrich Nietzsche (1844-1900)

"There are no facts, only interpretations."

"Why does man not see things? He is himself standing in the way: he conceals things."

The above-mentioned quotations are given by Friedrich Nietzsche, a German philosopher. His primary ideas include perspectivism, the eternal recurrence, truth and knowledge, values and morals, contemporary culture and the will to power, philosophy and science.

Thus Spoke Zarathustra: A Book for All and None, a philosophical novel by Nietzsche and composed in four parts between 1883 and 1885, is described by Nietzsche himself as "the deepest ever written" . The book is a dense and esoteric treatise on philosophy and morality, featuring as protagonist a fictionalized prophet descending from his recluse to mankind, Zarathustra.

"Zarathustra" , presented in the prologue, is the denomination of human beings as a transition between apes and the "overman" . The overman is one of the many interconnecting, interdependent themes of the story, and is represented through several different metaphors. The symbol of the overman alludes to Nietzsche's notions of "self-management" , "self-instruction" , and "self-retrospection" . Expostulating these concepts, Zarathustra declares:

"I teach you the overman. Man is something that shall be overcome. What have you done to overcome him?"

"All beings so far have created something beyond themselves; and do you want to be the ebb of this great flood and even go back to the beasts rather than overcome man? What is the ape to man? A laughing stock or a painful embarrassment. And man shall be just that for the overman: a laughing stock or a painful embarrassment. You have made your way from worm to man, and much in you is still worm. Once you were apes, and even now, too, man is more ape than any ape."

"Whoever is the wisest among you is also a mere conflict and cross between plant and ghost. But do I bid you become ghosts or plants?"

"Behold, I teach you the overman! The overman is the meaning of the earth. Let your will say: the overman shall be the meaning of the earth! I beseech you, my brothers, remain faithful to the earth, and do not believe those who speak to you of otherworldly hopes! Poison-mixers are they, whether they know it or not. Despisers of life are they, decaying and poisoned themselves, of whom the earth is weary: so let them go!"

The book embodies innovative poetical and rhetorical methods of expression. It serves as a parallel to the various philosophical ideas present in Nietzsche's body of work. He has, however, said that "among my writings my Zarathustra stands to my mind by itself." Emphasizing its centrality and its status as his magnum opus, it is stated by Nietzsche that:

"With ("Thus Spoke Zarathustra") I have given mankind the greatest present that has ever been made to it so far. This book, with a voice bridging centuries, is not only the highest book there is, the book that is truly characterized by the air of the heights-the whole fact of man lies beneath it at a tremendous distance-it is also the deepest, born out of the innermost wealth of truth, an inexhaustible well to which no pail descends without coming up again filled with gold and goodness."

With the book, Nietzsche embraced a distinct aesthetic assiduity. He later reformulated many of his ideas, in his book Beyond Good and Evil and various other writings that he composed thereafter. He continued to emphasize his philosophical concerns; generally, his intention was to show an alternative to repressive moral codes.

Key words: Thus Spoke Zarathustra, perspectivism

Reference(s):

1. Nachlass, Nietzsche, trans. A. Danto translation
2. Daybreak, Nietzsche, trans. R.J. Hollingdale
3. Thus Spoke Zarathustra, Prologue, trans. Walter Kaufmann
4. Ecce Homo, Preface, trans. Walter Kaufmann

Jean-Jacques Rousseau (1712-1778)

"I have begun on a work which is without precedent, whose accomplishment will have no imitator. I propose to set before my fellow-mortals a man in all the truth of nature; and this man shall be myself."

And this man's name is Jean-Jacques Rousseau, who was born on June 28, 1712 in Geneva, Switzerland. Rousseau was a philosopher, writer, and composer of 18th-century Romanticism. His political philosophy heavily influenced the French Revolution, as well as the American Revolution and the overall development of modern political, sociological and educational thought.

Rousseau's profound insight can be found in almost every trace of modern philosophy today and his general philosophy tried to grasp an emotional and passionate side of man which he felt was left out of most previous philosophical thinking.

Rousseau's writing, Discourse on the Arts and Sciences (1750), contended that the advancement of art and science had not been beneficial to human beings. He argued that the progress of knowledge had made governments more powerful, and crushed individual liberty. He concluded that material progress had weakened the possibility of sincere friendship, replacing it with jealousy, trepidation and suspicion.

Rousseau was one of the first modern philosophers to attack the institution of private property, and therefore is considered a forebear of modern socialism and Communism. Rousseau also questioned the assumption that the will of the majority is always correct.

One of the primary principles of Rousseau's political philosophy is that politics and morality should not be separated. His ideas about education have profoundly influenced modern educational theory. He minimizes the importance of book learning, and recommends that a child's emotions should be educated before his reason. He placed a special emphasis on learning by experience.

Key words: education, learning by experience, society, morality

Reference(s):

1. The Confessions of Jean-Jacques Rousseau, Jean-Jacques Rousseau, trans. W. Conyngham Mallory

Francis Bacon (1561-1626)

Francis Bacon was one of the noted figures in philosophy and in the field of scientific methodology. An English lawyer, member of Parliament, Queen's Counsel, essayist, historian, intellectual reformer, philosopher and champion of modern science, Bacon wrote on questions of law, politics and philosophy; he also published texts in which he speculated on possible conceptions of society, and he pondered questions of ethics even in his works on natural philosophy.

After graduation from Trinity College, Cambridge and Gray's Inn, London, Bacon chose to start a political career. Bacon's international fame and influence spread during his last years during the era of James I when he was able to focus his studies exclusively on his philosophical work. He proposed that all knowledge as his province and dedicated himself to a comprehensive revaluation and re-structuring of traditional learning.

To the present day, Bacon is distinguished for his works on empiricist natural philosophy and he is called the "father of empiricism" . His works has founded an inductive methodology for scientific inquiry, commonly called the Baconian method, or the scientific method, which focuses on a planned procedure of studying all matters. This method is regarded as a new turn in the theoretical framework for science.

Key words: learning, empiricist natural philosophy

Reference(s):

1. http://www.psychology.sbc.edu/Empiricism

Section IV: Artists

Leonardo da Vinci (1452-1519)

Leonardo da Vinci was a man of "both" worlds. He was a master of both of art and science. The Italian polymath was a painter, sculptor, architect, musician, engineer, mathematician, inventor, anatomist, botanist, writer and scientist. He is considered to be one of the greatest painters of all time and perhaps the most diversely talented person ever to have lived. Art historian Helen Gardner commended that the scope and depth of Leonardo da Vinci's interests were without precedent and "his mind and personality seem to us superhuman, the man himself mysterious and remote".

Leonardo was and is eminent primarily as a painter. Two of his works, the Mona Lisa and The Last Supper, are the most famous, most reproduced portrait and religious paintings of all time, respectively. Leonardo's drawing of the Vitruvian Man is also regarded as a cultural icon, being reproduced on everything from the Euro to text books to t-shirts.

Leonardo is also venerated for his technological ingenuity. He conceptualized a helicopter, a tank, concentrated solar power, a calculator, the double hull and outlined a rudimentary theory of plate tectonics. As a scientist, he greatly advanced the state of knowledge in the fields of anatomy, engineering and optics.

Many of his texts including "A well-spent day brings happy sleep," "Art is never finished, only abandoned," and "I love those who can smile in trouble, who can gather strenght from distress, and grow brave by reflection" still encourage people today to be retrospective and persistent.

Key words: reflection, ingenuity, invention

Reference(s):

1. Gardner, Helen, Art through the Ages (1970)

Michelangelo (1475-1564)

Michelangelo once said that he was no painter; on another occasion he declared he was no architect, but in reality he was both.

Michelangelo's output in both fields during his life was prodigious; he is the best-documented artist of the 16th century. Two of his best-known works, the "Pietà" and "David", were sculpted before he turned thirty. Michelangelo also created two of the most influential works in fresco in the history of Western art: the scenes from Genesis on the ceiling and The Last Judgment on the altar wall of the Sistine Chapel in Rome.

Several anecdotes reveal that Michelangelo's skill, especially in sculpture, was admired in his own time. One day, Michelangelo saw a beautiful marble in a stone market. He went to the storekeeper and asked for the price. The storekeeper said, "If you want to take it, just take it; it's free for you since it's been here for a long time and it's waste of my space. For the past twelve years, no one even asked about it; I don't see any value in it." So Michelangelo took the stone home.

He spent almost a year working on this marble and finally produced a statue of Jesus Christ who was lying in his mother Mary's arms after taking off the cross. The sculpture was so vivid that Jesus Christ seemed to wake up at any time.

Michelangelo then invited the storekeeper to see his work. The storekeeper couldn't believe what he saw. He said, "Where did you get such a beautiful marble?" Michelangelo replied, "From you. Didn't you recognize that this is the ugly stone in front of your store?" The storekeeper was suprised and asked Michelangelo how he did it. Michelangelo said, "What I did is nothing important; I simply removed the unnecessary part of the stone."

The high point of Michelangelo's style is the gigantic marble "David", which he produced between 1501 and 1504 in Florence. The character of David and what he symbolizes, was perfectly in tune with Michelangelo's patriotic feelings. At the time, Florence was going through a difficult period, and its citizens had to confront permanent threats. He used David as a model of heroic courage, in the hope that the Florentines would understand his message. This young Biblical hero demonstrated that inner spiritual strength can prove to be more effective than arms.

Michelangelo wrote in his diaries: "When I returned to Florence, I found myself famous. The City Council asked me to carve a colossal David from a nineteen-foot block of marble-and damaged to boot! I locked myself away in a workshop behind the cathedral, hammered and chiseled at the towering block for three long years. In spite of the opposition of a committee of fellow artists, I insisted that the figure should stand before the Palazzo Vecchio, as a symbol of our Republic. I had my way. Archways were torn down, narrow streets widened...it took forty men five days to move it. Once in place, all Florence was astounded. A civic hero, he was a warning...whoever governed Florence should govern justly and defend it bravely. Eyes watchful...the neck of a bull...hands of a killer...the body, a reservoir of energy. He stands poised to strike."

In his personal life, Michelangelo was abstemious. He once said to his apprentice, Ascanio Condivi: "However rich I may have been, I have always lived like a poor man." Condivi said ate "more out of necessity than of pleasure" and that he "often slept in his clothes." His biographer Paolo Giovio said, "His nature was so rough and uncouth that his domestic habits were incredibly squalid, and deprived posterity of any pupils who might have followed him." He may not have minded, since he was by nature a solitary person. He had a reputation for being bizzare because he "withdrew himself from the company of men."

Key words: prodigious, solitary, melancholy

Reference(s):

1. Early Life, http://www.michelangelo.com
2. Condivi, The life of Michelangelo
3. Paola Barocchi (ed), Scritti d'arte del cinquecento, Milan, 1971; vol. I
4. Condivi, The Life of Michelangelo

Vincent van Gogh (1853-1890)

Van Gogh, for whom color was the chief symbol of expression, was a Dutch painter whose work had a far-reaching influence on 20th century art.

The son of a pastor, brought up in a religious and cultured family, Van Gogh didn't decide to become an artist until his late twenties. He produced more than 2,000 artworks, including about 900 paintings and 1,100 drawings and sketches. Today many of his paintings such as his self portraits, sunflowers, and landscapes are among the world's most recognizable and expensive works of art. However, Van Gogh had sold one painting.

Yes. Van Gogh created thirty-seven self portaits in his lifetime. He was a prolific self portraitist.

Van Gogh's several versions of landscapes with flowers, as seen in View of Arles with Irises, and paintings of flowers, such as Irises, Sunflowers, lilacs, roses, and other flowers, reflect his interests in the language of color. He finished two series of sunflowers: the first when he was in Paris in 1887, and the second during his stay in Arlesin 1888. The first series shows living flowers in the ground. In the second series, they are dying in vases.

In a 1888 letter to his friend, he wrote, "I am hard at it, painting with the enthusiasm of a Marseillais eating bouillabaisse, which won't surprise you when you know that what I'm at is the painting of some sunflowers. If I carry out this idea there will be a dozen panels. So the whole thing will be a symphony in blue and yellow. I am working at it every morning from sunrise on, for the flowers fade so quickly. I am now on the fourth picture of sunflowers. This fourth one is a bunch of 14 flowers ... it gives a singular effect." The series is perhaps his best known and most widely reproduced.

During his lifetime, Van Gogh suffered from anxiety and mental illness, and died at the age of 37, from a self-inflicted gunshot wound.

Little appreciated throughout his lifetime, his fame grew quickly in the years after his death. Today, he is regarded as one of history's greatest painters.

Key words: expressionism, color

Reference(s):

1. Sunflowers 1888, National Gallery, London

Johann Sebastian Bach (1685-1750)

The son of Johann Ambrosius, court trumpeter for the Duke of Eisenach and director of the musicians of the town of Eisenach in Thuringia, Germany, Johann Sebastian Bach was born on March 21, 1685. For many years, members of the Bach family throughout Thuringia had held positions including organists and town instrumentalists.

As a distinguished composer, organist, and violinist, Bach enriched German music style with a robust contrapuntal technique, an unrivalled control of harmonic and motivic organization, and the adaptation of rhythms and forms from abroad such as Italy and France.

At an early age Bach lost a sister and later a brother. When he was only nine years old his mother died. Barely nine months later his father also died. Johann Sebastian and one of his brothers, Johann Jakob, were taken into the home of their eldest brother, Johann Christoph.

Bach's access to musicians, scores and instruments as a child and a young man, combined with his talent for writing tightly woven music of powerful sonority, have set him on course to develop an eclectic, energetic musical style. The period between 1713 and 1714, when a large repertoire of Italian music became available to the Weimar court orchestra, was a turning point to Bach. From this time on, he had absorbed into his style the Italians' dramatic openings, clear melodic contours, the sharp outlines of their bass lines, greater rhythmic conciseness, more unified motivic treatment, and more clearly articulated schemes for modulation.

Bach's works primarily include The Brandenburg Concertos, The Goldberg Variations, The Mass in B Minor, The Well-Tempered Clavier, The Partitas, The

Magnificat, TheMusical Offering, more than 200 cantatas, and a similar number of organ works, including the celebrated Toccata and Fugue in D minor and Passacaglia and Fugue in C minor.

Bach's abilities as an organist were highly revered in Europe throughout his lifetime although he was not recognized as a great composer until a revival of performances of his music in the first half of the 19th century. He is now regarded as the supreme composer of the Baroque, and as one of the greatest of all time.

Key words: intellectual depth, technical command and artistic beauty

Reference(s):

1. Wolff, Christoph, Johann Sebastian Bach: The Learned Musician (2000)

2. Blanning, T. C. W., The Triumph of Music: the Rise of Composers, Musicians and Their Art

Charlie Chaplin (1889-1977)

Sir Charles Spencer, also known as Charlie Chaplin, was an English comic actor and film director of the silent film era. The American Film Institute named Chaplin the 10th greatest male screen legend of all time. Martin Sieff, in a review of the book Chaplin: A Life, wrote: "Chaplin was not just 'big', he was gigantic. In 1915, he burst onto a war-torn world bringing it the gift of comedy, laughter and relief while it was tearing itself apart through the First World War. Over the next 25 years, through the Great Depression and the rise of Hitler, he stayed on the job. It is doubtful any individual has ever given more entertainment, pleasure and relief to so many human beings when they needed it the most." George Bernard Shaw said Chaplin was "the only genius to come out of the movie industry."

Chaplin's primary works include: The Gold Rush, City Lights, Modern Times, and The Great Dictator.

One of the most creative and influential personalities of the silent-film era, Chaplin was influenced by the French silent movie comedian Max Linder, to whom he dedicated one of his films. His career in entertainment spanned more than 75 years, from the Victorian stage and the Music Hall in the United Kingdom as a child actor, until close to his death at the age of 88. His high-profile public and private life encompassed both admiration and controversy.

Key words: silent film, the Great Depression

Reference(s):

1. AFI's 100 YEARS...100 STARS, American Film Institute, Jun. 16, 1999

2. Martin Sieff, Washington Times-Books, Dec. 21, 2008

3. John Walsh, The Big Question: Does Charlie Chaplin merit a museum in his honour, and what is his legacy?

Section V: Authors

Dante Alighieri (1265-1321)

An exiled figure throughout his lifetime, Dante is now considered the greatest Italian poet and one of the most important writers of European literature.

Dante's Divine Comedy, considered the greatest literary work in Italy and a masterpiece of world literature, is the story of a journey through Hell, Purgatory and Paradise. In the poem, the first two phases are guided by the Roman poet Virgil, and the visit to Paradise is led by Beatrice, a girl Dante met when he was nine and whom he adored the rest of his life. The Divine Comedy is the "source of a number of famous classical images, inspiring works by William Blake and many others." The Divine Comedy has also largely affected not only the religious imagination but all creation of imaginary worlds in literature.

Key words: Divine Comedy

William Shakespeare (1564-1616)

An English poet and playwright, William Shakespeare was widely regarded as the greatest writer in the English language and one of the most extraordinary creators in human history. During England's Elizabethan period, he wrote 38 plays, 154 sonnets, two long narrative poems, and some other poems, which continue to dominate world theater and readers 400 hundred years later.

Shakespeare handled drama and romance comedy with equal ease, and so famous are his texts that his quotes, from "To be or not to be" to "There is nothing either good or bad, but thinking makes it so" , take up more than 70 pages in recent editions of John Bartlett's A Collection of Familiar Quotations.

Shakespeare was born and raised in Stratford-upon-Avon, and many of his plays were originally performed in the Globe Theater in London. Among his best-known plays are Romeo and Juliet, Hamlet, MacBeth, Julius Caesar, King Lear, Othello, Henry IV, All 's Well That Ends Well, As You Like It, The Merry Wives of Windsor, The Merchant of Venice, A Midsummer Night 's Dream, The Tempest, Twelfth Night, and Much Ado About Nothing.

Shakespeare was a revered playwright and poet in his own day, but his fame and reputation did not rise to its present heights until the 19th century. His plays remain highly popular today and are constantly studied, performed and reinterpreted in various cultural contexts throughout the world.

Key words: poet, playwright, greatest

Reference(s):

1. John Bartlett, A Collection of Familiar Quotations

Ralph Waldo Emerson (1803-1882)

"A man of genius is privileged only as far as he is genius. His dullness is as insupportable as any other dullness."

"All our progress is an unfolding, like a vegetable bud. You have first an instinct, then an opinion, then a knowledge as the plant has root, bud, and fruit. Trust the instinct to the end, though you can render no reason."

"A man of genius is privileged only as far as he is genius. His dullness is as insupportable as any other dullness."

The above well-known quotations are given by Ralph Waldo Emerson. One of America's most influential authors, philosophers and thinkers, Emerson was influenced by a number of European intellectuals including William Wordsworth, Thomas Carlyle and Plato. On Sept. 9, 1836, Emerson anonymously expressed transcendentalism's principle of the "mystical unity of nature" in his essay, Nature. In 1837 he delivered the famous Phi Beta Kappa address, "An Oration, Delivered before the Phi Beta Kappa Society at Cambridge" (now known as "The American Scholar"); it was renamed for a collection of essays in 1849. In the speech, Emerson claimed literary independence in the United States and urged Americans to "create a writing style all their own and free from Europe". Emerson also declared that a scholar learns best by engaging life. James Russell Lowell, who was a student at Harvard during that time, said it was "an event without former parallel on our literary annals"; Reverend John Pierce, also one of the members in the audience called it "an apparently incoherent and unintelligible address".

Key words: nature, engaging life

Reference(s):

1. Peter Watson, Ideas: A History of Thought and Invention, from Fire to Freud. New York: Harper Perennial

2. R. B. Mowat, The Victorian Age. London: Senate

3. Louis Menand, The Metaphysical Club: A Story of Ideas in America. New York: Farrar, Straus and Giroux

Mark Twain (1835-1910)

"Banker is a fellow who lends you his umbrella when the sun is shining, but wants it back the minute it begins to rain."

"Courage is resistance to fear, mastery of fear-not absence of fear."

"Do something every day that you don't want to do; this is the golden rule for acquiring the habit of doing your duty without pain."

Lauded as the "greatest American humorist of his age" , and the "father of American literature" , Samuel Clemens (pen name Mark Twain) is considered the greatest humorist of the 19th century American literature. His well-known novels including The Adventures of Tom Sawyer and The Adventures of Huckleberry Finn are still popular today.

After an unsuccessful attempt at gold mining he joined the staff of a newspaper in Virginia City, Nevada in 1863. Staring from that time, he wrote under the pen name, Mark Twain.

He then traveled as a reporter for a number of newspapers. In 1869 his travel letters from Europe were collected into the book, The Innocents Abroad. A few years later, he settled down in Hartford, Connecticut to his most productive years as a writer. Between 1873 and 1889 he wrote seven novels including the two "Adventures" books, The Prince and the Pauper and A Connecticut Yankee in King Arthur's Court.

Twain used contemporary and colloquial language in his books to bring his characters to life, which influenced many young writers in America. As Twain's career progressed he became increasingly cynical and doubtful, losing much of the humorous tone of his earlier years. Even so Twain is best remembered as a humorist who used his astute wit and bold exaggeration to attack the fakeness, arrogance and egoism he saw in humanity.

Key words: humorist, little formal school

Reference(s):

1. Robert A. Jelliffe, Faulkner at Nagano (1956)Italo Calvino (1923-1985)

Italo Calvino, one of Italy's greatest writers of short stories and novels, has influenced readers around the world with his simple, fable-like stories. His major works include the Our Ancestors trilogy, Cosmicomics, the novels Invisible Cities and If on a winter 's night a traveler.

The son of botanists, Calvino was born in Cuba in 1923 and raised in San Remo, Italy.

After taking a degree in literature from the University of Turin in 1947, Calvino became a journalist for a newspaper. Starting from 1960s, Calvino's writing gradually diverged from the neorealist style and assumed its own distinctive voice. He wrote: "My working method has more often than not involved the subtraction of weight. I have tried to remove weight, sometimes from people, sometimes from heavenly bodies, sometimes from cities; above all I have tried to remove weight from the structure of stories and from language."

During his later years, Calvino became a renown lecturer. But he went through what he called an "intellectual depression" . The writer himself described it as an important course in his life: "I ceased to be young. Perhaps it's a metabolic process, something that comes with age, I'd been young for a long time, perhaps too long, suddenly I felt that I had to begin my old age, yes, old age, perhaps with the hope of prolonging it by beginning it early." He died of a brain hemorrhage in Siena on Sept. 19, 1985.

Key words: neorealist style

Reference(s):

1. Italo Calvino, http://www.worldliteratureforum.com

Jules Verne (1828-1905)

Jules Gabriel Verne, often referred to as the Father of science fiction, was a French author who helped pioneer the science-fiction genre. His major works include Around the World in Eighty Days, A Journey to the Centre of the Earth,

From the Earth to the Moon, and Twenty Thousand Leagues Under the Sea, among which many have been made into films.

Jules Verne's novels have been noted for being astonishingly accurate anticipations of modern times. Many of his books have vivid descriptions of electricity, television, air conditioning, even the Internet, and other modern technologies which are similar to their real world counterparts. For instance, in his book, From the Earth to the Moon, which, except for using a space gun instead of a rocket, is incredibly similar to the real Apollo Program, as three astronauts are launched from Cape Canaveral, Florida and recovered through a tough landing. "In From the Earth to the Moon, the spacecraft is launched from Tampa, Florida, which is about 130 miles from the launching site. Verne also predicted the inventions of submarines, helicopters, projectors, and other later modern equipments."

Key words: predict, accurate anticipations of modern times

Reference(s):

1. Edmund J. Smyth, Jules Verne: Narratives of Modernity (2000)

Section VI: Humanitarians

Mother Teresa (1910-1997)

Mother Teresa has quietly devoted her life to the world's disadvantaged, spreading her message of courage and hope from the slums of India to AIDS clinics in the United States. In 1979, she received the Novel Peace Prize for her work with the poor around the world.

In 1927, she joined an Irish order, the Sisters of Loretto, which is known for their missionary work in India and during that time, she took the name Teresa.

In 1944, Mother Teresa became the principal of St. Mary's. On Sept. 10, 1946, she contracted tuberculosis, and was sent to Darjeeling for recuperation. It was on the train to Darjeeling that she received what she described as "the call within the call" . Mother Teresa recalled later, "I was to leave the convent and work with the poor, living among them. It was an order. To fail would have been to break the faith."

In the beginning of 1949, a group of her former pupils joined her and laid the foundations to create a new religious community helping the "poorest among the poor" . They found many men, women, and children dying on the streets who were rejected by hospitals. The group rented a room so they could take care of these helpless people. In1950, the group was established by the City of Calcutta, which was known as the Missionaries of Charity. Her efforts soon caught the attention of Indian officials, including the prime minister, who expressed his appreciation. Over the years, Mother Teresa's Missionaries of Charity grew from 12 to thousands. They provide help to the poorest of the poor in countries in Africa, Asia, and Latin America. The also provide rooms in America, and Europe, where take care of the homeless, alcoholics and AIDS victims. For about 45 years, Mother Teresa comforted the poor and dying around the world.

Mother Teresa gained reverence with her untiring efforts on behalf of world peace. By the 1970s, she was famed as a humanitarian and advocate for the helpless and the poor. She said, "Keep the joy of loving the poor and share this joy with all you meet. Remember works of love are works of Peace."

Key words: charity, advocate for the poor and helpless

References:

1. Joan Graff Clucas, Mother Teresa (1988)
2. Williams Paul, Mother Teresa (2002)
3. Peace 1901-1970, Nobel Lectures

Section VII: Scientists and inventors

Sir Isaac Newton (1642-1727)

One of the foremost mathematists and physicists of all time, Isaac Newton laid the foundations for modern science and revolutionized the world.

Newton was educated at Trinity College, Cambridge University in England. In 1666, the university was closed because of a plague. Newton then came to his family's estate in Lincolnshire, where an apple's falling to the ground is said to have inspired the 23-year-old scientist to develop his theory of gravitation. During the period from 1665 to 1666, Newton was at the height of his creative power and he later said that this period was "the prime of my age of invention." Newton invented integral calculus, and jointly with Leibnitz, differential calculus. He also made a huge impact on theoretical astronomy. He defined the laws of motion and universal gravitation which he used to predict precisely the motions of stars, and the planets around the sun.

Newton died on Mar. 20, 1727 and was buried in Westminster Abbey, the first scientist to be accorded this honor. Despite the considerable inventions, Newton remained remarkably humble. He said, "If I have been able to see further, it was only because I stood on the shoulders of giants."

Key words: apple, gravitation, invention, humble

Reference(s):

1. Letter from Isaac Newton to Robert Hooke, Feb. 1676, as transcribed in Jean-Pierre Maury (1992) Newton: Understanding the Cosmos, New Horizons

Charles Darwin (1809-1882)

Charles Darwin was a British naturalist who was distinguished for his theories of evolution and natural selection. His primary works, The Origin of Species by Means of Natural Selection and The Descent of Man marked a new epoch.

In the book The Origin of Species by Means of Natural Selection, Darwin set forth his theory of evolutionary selection which holds that variation within species occurs randomly and that the survival or extinction of each organism is determined by that organism's ability to adapt to its environment. After the publication of the book, many people strongly opposed the idea of evolution; they thought the new concept conflicted with their religious convictions.

Darwin wrote in the book: "It may be said that natural selection is daily and hourly scrutinizing, throughout the world, every variation, even the slightest; rejecting that which is bad, preserving and adding up all that is good; silently and insensibly working, whenever and wherever opportunity offers, at the improvement of each organic being in relation to its organic and inorganic conditions of life. We see nothing of these slow changes in progress, until the hand of time has marked the long lapses of ages, and then so imperfect is our view into long past geological ages, that we only see that the forms of life are now different from what they formerly were."

Darwin's idea has never been successfully refuted. Without any doubt, Darwin's evolutionary vision is a monistic one; it shows that the universe is a continuous process. Julian Huxley, grandson of Thomas H. Huxley who was an English biologist an a defender of Darwin, said, Darwin's idea is "the most powerful and the most comprehensive idea that has ever arisen on earth. It helps us understand our origins ... We are part of a total process, made of the same matter and operating by the same energy as the rest of the cosmos, maintaining and reproducing by the same type of mechanism as the rest of life."

Key words: evolution, natural selection, origin of species

Reference(s):

1. Charles Darwin, Natural Selection
2. Julian Huxley, Evolutionary Humanism Buffalo

Albert Einstein (1879-1955)

Albert Einstein was regarded as one of the most influential scientists of all time. He published more than 300 scientific works and his major works on physics include Special Theory of Relativity, Relativity, General Theory of Relativity, Investigations on Theory of Brownian Movement, and The Evolution of Physics. Einstein was also a philosopher and a writer; he wrote numerous philosophical and political topics. His non-scientific works primarily include About Zionism, Why War?, My Philosophy, and Out of My Later Years.

His contributions to physics mainly include "the special and general theories of relativity, the founding of relativistic cosmology, the first post-Newtonian expansion, explaining the perihelion advance of Mercury, prediction of the deflection of light by gravity and gravitational lensing, the photon theory and wave-particle duality, the quantum theory of atomic motion in solids, the first fluctuation dissipation theorem which explained the Brownian movement of molecules, the zero- point energy concept, and the quantum theory of a monatomic gas which predicted Bose-Einstein condensation."

Einstein received honorary doctorate degrees in science and medicine from many American and European universities. He gained a number of awards in recognition of his work, including the Copley Medal of the Royal Society of London, and the Franklin Medal of the Franklin Institute. In 1921 he received Nobel Prize in Physics "for his services to Theoretical Physics, and especially for his discovery of the law of the photoelectric effect" .

Isaac Newton established the theory of gravitation inspired by an falling apple. Likewise, Einstein built his theory of relativity by seizing on an insight that occurred to him in1907, when he was 28. According to his own account, he said, "I was sitting on a chair in my patent office in Bern. Suddenly a thought struck me: If a man falls freely, he would not feel his weight. I was taken aback. This simple thought experiment made a deep impression on me." By linking accelerated motion and gravity, Einstein created his masterwork, the general theory of relativity.

Key words: relativity, inspiration, philosophy

Reference(s):

1. Albert Einstein, Wikipedia, the free encyclopedia

2. Physics, Nobel Lectures (1901-1921)

3. Albert Einstein, Encyclopedia Britannica

Thomas Edison (1847-1931)

Thomas Edison was an American inventor and scientist who developed thousands of devices that deeply influenced life around the world. He is a prolific inventor, holding 1,093 U.S. patents in his name, among which, the long-lasting and practical electric light bulb greatly changed human existence by bringing light to the night and making it hospitable to human activities.

Edison was not the first one who came up with the idea of illuminating the night. The first electric light was made in 1809 by Humphry Davy, an English scientist. He "connected wires and a piece of carbon to a battery, and the carbon glowed, producing light" . About 70 years later, Herman Sprengel invented the mercury vacuum pump making it possible to "develop a practical electric light bulb by making a really good vacuum inside the bulb possible" . In 1878, English scientist Sir Joseph Wilson Swan invented the first practical electric light bulb which could last 13.5 hours. Swan "used a carbon fiber filament derived from cotton."

However, it is Thomas Edison who contributed to the perfection of this device. He and his team experimented with thousands of various filaments to find just the right material to glow well and be long-lasting. In 1879 Edison made a breakthrough ; "he discovered that a carbon filament in an oxygen-free bulb glowed for 40 hours." Soon, "by changing the shape of the filament to a horseshoe it burned for more than 100 hours and later, by numerous improvements, it lasted for 1500 hours."

For his success of the invention of light bulb, Edison remained humble, claiming that "I have not failed. I've just found $10,000$ ways that won't work" . and that "Invention was 1 percent inspiration and 99 percent perspiration."

Edison only attended school for three months, in Port Huron, Michigan. When he was 12 years old he started to sell newspapers on the Grand Trunk Railway, devoting much of his spare time mainly to experimentation with electrical and mechanical apparatus.

Thomas Edison died on Oct. 18, 1931, at his home, Glenmont in Llewellyn Park in West Orange, New Jersey. "The great inventor, the fruits of whose genius so magically transformed the everyday world, was 84 years and 8 months old."

Key words: prolific, 1093 patents, inspiration, perspiration

Reference(s):

1. The Invention of the Light Bulb: Davy, Swan and Edison, nchantedLearning. com

2. Fascinating Facts about the Invention of the Light Bulb, The Great Idea Finder

3. Thomas Edison Dies in Coma at 84, New York Times. (Oct. 18, 1931)

Marie Curie (1867-1934)

Marie Sk?odowska Curie was a physicist and chemist of Polish upbringing and subsequent French citizenship. She was a pioneer in the field of radioactivity and the first person honored with two Nobel Prizes, one in physics and another in chemistry. She was also the first female professor at the University of Paris. Her major achievements are: "the creation of a theory of radioactivity (a term she coined), techniques for isolating radioactive isotopes, and the discovery of two new elements, polonium and radium. Under her direction, the world's first studies were conducted into the treatment of neoplasms (cancers) using radioactive isotopes."

Key words: honored with two Nobel Prizes, radioactivity

Reference(s):

1. Nobel Prize Facts, http://www.nobelprize.org
2. Robert Reid, Marie Curie

Section VIII: Leaders

Mohandas Karamchand Gandhi (1869-1948)

Known as "Great Soul" , Mohandas Karamchand Gandhi was the leader of the India during the national independence movement, and his philosophy of non-violent protest to achieve political and social development has been greatly influential. The philosophy of non-violence not only helped India to independence, but inspired movements for civil rights and freedom around the world. His birthday, Oct., 2, is commemorated in India as a national holiday, and worldwide as the International Day of Non-Violence.

Gandhi was a lawyer at an Indian law firm in Durban, South Africa in 1893. He was shocked by the treatment of Indian immigrants there. So he joined the struggle to obtain rights for them. During his years in South Africa, he was sent to prison many times. It was also during those years, Gandhi developed the non-violent way to redress wrongs. In 1914, the South African government conceded to many of Gandhi's demands. In 1915, Ganhdi organized protests by farmers and urban laborers concerning excessive tax and discrimination. In 1921, he was assumed the leader of the Indian National Congress. He led nationwide movements to ease poverty and expand women's rights. In particular, he led his followers in the peaceful non-cooperation movement that protested the British-imposed salt tax, "leading thousands on a 'March to the Sea' to symbolically make their own salt from seawater." In 1942, he launched the civil disobedience movement demanding immediate independence for India.

"Gandhi lived modestly in a self-sufficient residential community" . He ate vegetarian food, "experimented for a time with a fruitarian diet, and undertook long fasts as a means of both self-purification and social protest." On Jan. 30, 1948, he was assassinated in Delhi by a Hindu fanatic.

Key words: non-violence

Reference(s):

1. Mohandas Gandhi, http://www.bbc.co.uk/history

George Washington (1732-1799)

George Washington was the first President of the United States from 1789 to 1797. Because of his significant role in the American Revolutionary War from 1775 to 1783 and in the formation of the United States of America, he is respected by Americans as the "Father of the Country" .

Here is a story of George Washington when he was at age six. One day, while he was playing in the garden, he noticed a cherry tree, which his father planted. During that time, like many other little boys, he liked to use a hatchet to chop everything that came in his way. So he tried the edge of his hatchet on the trunk of the tree and barked it; the cherry tree finally died. His father was so angry that he came into the house and asked who had cut away the bark. Nobody answered. Just then George came into the room. His father then turned to George and asked if he knew who killed his cherry tree. George realized that he made a big mistake and said, "I cannot tell a lie, Pa, you know I cannot tell a lie! I did cut it with my little hatchet." Hearing what George has said, his father calmed down and said: "My son, that you should not be afraid to tell the truth is more to me than a thousand trees! Yes. Though they were blossomed with silver and had leaves of the purest gold!"

"This story was first reported by biographer Parson Weems, who after Washington's death interviewed people who knew him as a child. The Weems' version was widely reprinted throughout the 19th century. Many parents wanted their children to learn moral lessons from the past from history, especially as taught by great national heroes like Washington."

Washington's success during the Independence War made him a revered figure in America. He was the natural choice to serve as America's first president in 1789. He served two terms, refused a third, and returned to his Virginia farm.

Key words: "I cannot tell a lie" , cherry tree, Father of America

Reference(s):

1. M. Weems, The Cherry Tree, Legends and Short Stories of George Washington

Abraham Lincoln (1809-1865)

"...that we here highly resolve that these dead shall not have died in vain, that this nation under God shall have a new birth freedom, and that government of the people, by the people, for the people shall not perish from the earth."

The Gettysburg Address, one of the most quoted political speeches in history, was delivered at the dedication of the Soldiers' National Cemetery in Gettysburg, Pennsylvania on Nov. 19, 1863, during the American Civil War, four and a half months after the Battle of Gettysburg. In this 272-word short speech, Abraham Lincoln declared the country was born, in 1776, but not in 1789 , "conceived in liberty, and dedicated to the proposition that all men are created equal." He claimed the war as an effort dedicated to liberty and equality. He said that the deaths of numerous soldiers would not be in vain, that slavery would end as a result of the losses, and the future of democracy would be assured. He concluded that the Civil War had a profound objective- a new founding of the nation.

Lincoln was elected president of America in 1861. He introduced measures that end slavery, and that preserves America as a Union by defeating the secessionist Confederate States of America in the American Civil War. In April, 1965, six days after the surrender of Confederate forces, Lincoln was assassinated. He has been ranked as one of the greatest of all American Presidents.

Key words: liberty, equality, American Civil War, ending slavery

Reference(s):

1. Roy P. Basler (ed), Collected Works of Abraham Lincoln

2. David Herbert Donald, Lincoln

3. Garry Wills, Lincoln at Gettysburg: The Words That Remade America

Napoleon Bonaparte (1769-1821)

The famous quote, "A throne is only a bench covered with velvet," was written by Napoleon Bonaparte, also known as Napoleon I, who was considered as one of the greatest military and political leaders of France. His military efforts and actions dominated Europe for about ten years in the early 19th century.

Born to parents of Italian ancestry, he was educated in France and became an army officer in 1785. He fought in the French Revolutionary Wars and was promoted to brigadier general in 1793. In 1804, the French Senate proclaimed Bonaparte emperor. He maintained the influence of France through building many alliances, and by which he ruled other European countries as French client states.

Napoleon made mistakes and suffered setbacks, too. His army was badly damaged in the French invasion of Russia in 1812 and never recovered. In 1815, Napoleon was defeated at the Battle of Waterloo, one of the best known battles in history. In fact, either side could have won, but Napoleon's "arrogance, and mistakes in communication, leadership and judgement ultimately led to French defeat", which also ended Napoleon's hundred days' reign. He was exiled to the island of St. Helena where he died in 1821.

Key words: arrogance, Battle of Waterloo

Reference(s):

1. Why did Napopleon lose? The battle of Waterloo, http://www. bbc.co.uk/history

Section IX: Businessmen

Henry Ford (1863-1947)

American industrialist and pioneer automobile manufacturer, Henry Ford created the first inexpensive mass assembly lines used in mass production, which revolutionized transportation and American industry.

Ford began his working life as a machinist's apprentice at age 15 and then became a chief engineer at the Edison Company in Detroit. He created his first experimental four-wheeled car with a gasoline engine in 1896. In 1903, he founded the Ford Motor Company with a few friends. In 1908, he introduced the Model T. Because the demand was so great that "Ford developed new mass production methods, including the first moving assembly line in 1913. He developed the Model A in 1928 to replace the Model T, and in 1932 he introduced the V-8 engine." "By 1924, 10 million Model T cars had been sold and Detroit become the auto-making capital of America." After his death in 1947, most of Ford's vast wealth was used to create the philanthropic Ford Foundation.

Key words: assembly line, philanthropic

Reference(s):

1. Henry Ford, Britannica Concise Encyclopedia
2. Henry Ford, Who2 Biographies

Bill Gates (1955-)

"Your most unhappy customers are your greatest source of learning." -The text is written by Bill Gates, one of the most influential businessmen in the world.

Bill Gates is an American business magnate, philanthropist, and chairman of Microsoft, co-founded with Paul Allen. He is also the world's richest person for many years, according to Forbes magazine.

Gates' score on the SAT was 1590 out of 1600. He began to study at Harvard

University in 1973. While at Harvard, he spent most of his spare time with Allen, working on a version of the programming language, Basic. In 1975, the MITS Altair 8800 based on the Intel 8080 CPU was released. "Gates and Allen saw this as the opportunity to start their own computer software company."

Gates wanted to achieve his goal and he soon made a big decision to drop out of Harvard. People did not understand why he would give up such a good opportunity to study at one of the world's most famous universities during that time. After he left Harvard, Gates and Allen started the engine of Microsoft Corporation, which now dominates the computer market with its operating systems such as Windows, and becomes the largest computer software company in the world.

In 1994, after studying the work of Andrew Carnegie and John D. Rockefeller, Gates decided to give more of his wealth to charity. He then established the William H. Gates Foundation. Later in 2000, "Gates and his wife combined three family foundations into one to create the charitable Bill & Melinda Gates Foundation, which is the largest transparently operated charitable foundation in the world." As of 2007, Bill and Melinda Gates were the second most generous philanthropists in America, having given over US$28 billion to charity.

Key words: give up, drop out of Harvard, charity

Reference(s):

1. The new-and improved?-SAT, The Week Magazine (May 10, 2006)

2. The 50 Most Generous Philanthropists, http://www.businessweek.com

S.A.T Chapter VII

Quotes and Proverbs

　　恰當地引用名人名言或者格言警句，不僅可以昇華文章的主旨，而且還能給讀者以心靈的契合，其畫龍點睛的作用不可小覷。

Using quotes or proverbs appropriately in your essay would impress SAT essay graders. Undoubtedly, it's a trait that they love to reward. Now choose some quotes and proverbs that you love here and try to memorize them.

Education

**If a man empties his purse into his head, no man can take it away from him. An investment in knowledge always pays the best interest.

Benjamin Franklin, American statesman, scientist and philosopher.

**Education is a progressive discovery of our ignorance.

Durant, American historian.

**Education comes from within; you get it by struggle and effort and thought.

Napoleon Hill, American speaker and motivational writer.

**The roots of education are bitter, but the fruit is sweet.

Aristotle, Greek philosopher.

**I cannot teach anybody anything, I can only make them think.

Socrates, Greek philosopher of Athens.

**I am not a teacher, but an awakener.

Robert Frost, American Poet.

**Education is the ability to listen to almost anything without losing your temper oryour self-confidence.

Robert Frost, American Poet.

**The secret in education lies in respecting the student.

Ralph Waldo Emerson, American poet, essayist and lecturer.

Life

**Nothing in life is to be feared. It is only to be understood.

Marie Curie, French physicist.

**He that travels far knows much.

John Ray, British scientist.

**I never consider ease and joyfulness as the purpose of life itself.

Albert Einstein, American scientist.

**In almost every face and every person, they may discover fine feathers and defects, good and bad qualities.

Benjamin Franklin, American statesman, scientist and philosopher.

In three words I can sum up everything I've learned about life. It goes on.

Robert Frost, American Poet.

**Life may not be the party we hoped for, but while we're here we should dance.

Unknown source.

**Live a good, honorable life. Then when you get older and think back, you'll be able toenjoy it a second time.

Unknown source.

Virtue

**Virtue is bold, and goodness never fearful.

William Shakespeare, British poet and playwright.

**If I have been able to see further, it was only because I stood on the shoulders of giants.

Sir Issac Newton, British physicist.

**Try not to become a man of success but rather try to become a man of value.

Albert Einstein, American scientist.

**The ideals which have lighted my way, and time after time have given me new courage to face life cheerfully have been kindness, beauty and truth.

Albert Einstein, American scientist.

Adversity and failure

**A man who has committed a mistake and doesn't correct it is committing another mistake.

Confucius, Chinese philosopher.

**Brave men rejoice in adversity, just as brave soldiers triumph in war.

Lucius Annaeus Seneca, Roman philosopher and playwright.

**Adversity is the first path to truth.

Lord Byron, British poet.

**Sweet are the uses of adversity which, like the toad, ugly and venomous, wears yet a precious jewel in his head.

William Shakespeare, British poet and playwright.

**People don't fail, they give up.

Unknown source.

**Your failures won't hurt you until you start blaming them on others.

Unknown source.

**I have not failed. I've just found 10,000 ways that won't work.

Thomas Edison, American inventor.

**Our business in this world is not to succeed, but to continue to fail, in good spirits.

Robert Louis Stevenson, Scottish essayist, poet and novelist.

Aim and success

**The important thing in life is to have a great aim, and the determination to attain it.

Johann Wolfgang von Goethe, German poet, philosopher and dramatist.

**The secret of success is to do all you can do without thought of success.

Unknown Source.

**On the pinnacle of success man does not stand firm long.

Johann Wolfgang von Goethe, German poet, philospher and dramatist.

**The ladder of success is never crowded at the top.

Napoleon Hill, American speaker and motivational writer.

**You will find the key to success under the alarm clock.

Benjamin Franklin, American statesman, scientist and philosopher.

**We must accept finite disappointment, but we must never lose infinite hope.

Martin Luther King, Jr., American clergyman, activist, and leader in the African American civil rights movement.

**Don't believe that winning is really everything. It's more important to stand for something. If you don't stand for something, what do you win?

Lane Kirkland, American labor union leader.

**You have to believe in yourself. That's the secret of success.

Charles Chaplin, British comic actor.

**The people who get on in this world are the people who get up and look for circumstances they want, and if they cannot find them, make them.

Bernard Shaw, British playwright.

**A great man is always willing to be little.

Ralph Waldo Emerson, American poet, essayist and lecturer.

**The only limit to our realization of tomorrow will be our doubts of today.

Franklin Roosevelt, 32nd President of the United States of America.

**Although the world is full of suffering, it is full also of the overcoming of it.

Hellen Keller, American writer.

**I want to bring out the secrets of nature and apply them for the happiness of man. I don't know of any better service to offer for the short time we are in the world.

Thomas Edison, American inventor.

**The man who has made up his mind to win will never say "Impossible" .

Napoleon, military and political leader of France.

**It never will rain roses. When we want to have more roses we must plant trees.

G. Eliot, British novelist.

**Do not, for one repulse, forgo the purpose that you resolved to effort.

Shakespeare, British poet and playwright.

Knowledge

**To be proud of learning is the greatest ignorance.

Jeremy Taylor, American composer.

**Work banishes those three great evils: boredom, vice, and poverty.

Voltaire, French philosopher.

**Imagination is more important than knowledge.

Albert Einstein, American scientist.

**Knowledge is power.

Francis Bacon, British philosopher and author.

**Experience is not what happens to a man; it is what a man does with what happens to him.

Aldous Leonard Huxley, American writer.

**Histories make men wise; poems witty; the mathematics subtle; natural philosophy deep; moral grave; logic and rhetoric able to contend.

Francis Bacon, British philosopher and author.

Teamwork

**It is amazing how much you can accomplish when it doesn't matter who gets the credit.

Unknown source.

**Teamwork: Simply stated, it is less me and more we.

Unknown source.

**TEAM = Together Everyone Achieves More

Unknown source.

**Teamwork is the ability to work together toward a common vision. It is the fuel that allows common people to attain uncommon results.

Andrew Carnegie, Scottish-American industrialist, businessman.

**The whole is greater than the sum of the parts.

Unknown source.

**A successful team beats with one heart.

Unknown source.

**Teamwork divides the task and doubles the success.

Unknown source.

**People who work together will win, whether it be against complex football defenses, or the problems of modern society.

Vince Lombardi, American football coach.

**Everyone is needed, but no one is necessary.

Unknown source.

**If I could solve all the problems myself, I would.

Thomas Edison, when asked why he had a team of twenty-one assistants.

SAT 作文滿分攻略

作　　者：鐘莉 編著

發 行 人：黃振庭

出 版 者：崧博出版事業有限公司

發 行 者：崧燁文化事業有限公司

E-mail：sonbookservice@gmail.com

粉 絲 頁：https://www.facebook.com/
　　　　　sonbookss/

網　　址：https://sonbook.net/

地　　址：台北市中正區重慶南路一段六十一號八
　　　　　樓 815 室

Rm. 815, 8F., No.61, Sec. 1, Chongqing S. Rd.,
Zhongzheng Dist., Taipei City 100, Taiwan (R.O.C)

電　　話：(02)2370-3310

傳　　真：(02) 2388-1990

總 經 銷：紅螞蟻圖書有限公司

地　　址：台北市內湖區舊宗路二段 121 巷 19 號

電　　話：02-2795-3656

傳　　真：02-2795-4100

印　　刷：京峯彩色印刷有限公司（京峰數位）

國家圖書館出版品預行編目資料

SAT 作文滿分攻略 / 鐘莉 編著 .--
第一版 .-- 臺北市：崧燁文化發行，
2020.8
　面；　公分
POD 版
ISBN 978-957-735-990-2(平裝)

官網

臉書

定　　價：320 元

發行日期：2020 年 8 月第一版

◎本書以 POD 印製